THE WATER-CASTLE

PARTHIAN

LIBRARY OF WALES

Brenda Chamberlain was born in Bangor in 1912. In 1931 she went to train as a painter at the Royal Academy Schools in London and five years later, after marrying the artist-craftsman John Petts, settled near the village of Llanllechid, near Bethesda in Caernarfonshire. During the Second World War, while working as a guide searching Snowdonia for lost aircraft, she temporarily gave up painting in favour of poetry and worked, with her husband, on the production of the Caseg Broadsheets, a series of six which included poems by Dylan Thomas, Alun Lewis and Lynette Roberts. In 1947, her marriage ended, she went to live on Bardsey (Ynys Enlli), a small island off the tip of the Llŷn Peninsula, where she remained until 1961. After six years on the Greek island of Ydra, she returned to Bangor. She died there in 1971.

She described the rigours and excitements of her life on Bardsey in *Tide-race* (1962) and the island also inspired many of her paintings. Her book of poems, *The Green Heart* (1958), contains work that reflects her life in Llanllechid, on Bardsey and in Germany. Her German experiences are portrayed in her novel *The Water-Castle* (1964). *A Rope of Vines* was published in 1965; *Poems with Drawings* in 1969; and *Alun Lewis and the Making of the Caseg Broadsheets* in 1970.

THE WATER-CASTLE

BRENDA CHAMBERLAIN

PARTHIAN
LIBRARY OF WALES

Parthian
The Old Surgery
Napier Street
Cardigan
SA43 1ED
www.parthianbooks.com

The Library of Wales is a Welsh Government
initiative which highlights and celebrates Wales' literary
heritage in the English language.

Published with the financial support of
the Welsh Books Council.

www.thelibraryofwales.com

Series Editor: Dai Smith

The Water-Castle first published in 1964
© Brenda Chamberlain
Library of Wales edition 2012
All Rights Reserved

ISBN 978-1-908069-79-5

Cover Image: *Charles at Ménerbes* (1961) by Brenda Chamberlain

Printed and bound by Gwasg Gomer, Llandysul, Wales
Typeset by Elaine Sharples

British Library Cataloguing in Publication Data

A cataloguing record for this book is available from the British Library.

INTRODUCTION

In a 1947 review of Gwyn Jones's collection of stories, *The Buttercup Field*, published in *The Dublin Magazine*, Brenda Chamberlain confessed the need she felt to get 'through the narrow archway of the enchanted castle that is Wales into the no less enchanted universe outside, of which the castle and its inhabitants are part'. Published in the year in which she left the hills above Llanllechid, Caernarfonshire, to establish a home on Bardsey Island (Ynys Enlli), this expression of a desire to experience and respond imaginatively to a world beyond the local may seem more than a little ironic. What kind of spirit counsels escape from a moated castle only to choose an island – in the specific case of Bardsey, one often made inaccessible by a hazardous tide-race – as home? Chamberlain's friend Jonah Jones said that she arrived on Bardsey 'part-wounded in some way' after the breakdown of her marriage to the artist and engraver John Petts. Yet Chamberlain's poetry, prose and paintings, while acutely attuned to the shapes of her native landscape and culture (as her masterpiece of fabling autobiography, *Tide-race* (1962) proves), had always gestured beyond the protection – and incarceration – of the Welsh castle. The major published works of her final, fraught decade form part of a complex emotional geography of Europe, extending from Bardsey through post-war Germany and down to Greece and the Aegean, where she saw 'the Welsh sea' joining 'its fountain-head, the maternal middle ocean that hisses round promontories of pale-boned islands' (as she would write in *A Rope of Vines: Journal from a Greek Island* (1965), also available in the Library of Wales series).

It was in 1932 in her native Bangor that the twenty-year-old Chamberlain met Karl von Laer, a young student on a visit from Thuringia, the 'green heart' of Germany. So began what Chamberlain referred to at the beginning of the title sequence of her poetry collection, *The Green Heart* (1958), as her 'communication across "deep water"' with von Laer, whose pre-war letters would condition the imagery and emotional tenor of so much of her poetry. She described the exchange as a 'silent dialogue' that brought her 'so close to him' that despite their geographical separation, 'a similarity of temperament and nervous awareness caused the experience of one to become the property of both'. From the moment she met von Laer, Chamberlain's work can be seen to chart lines of communication and response over dividing bodies of water, and across controlled fronts and borders. The Second World War, during which von Laer fought for Germany on the Russian front, temporarily broke that communication, but in late 1952, Chamberlain, accompanied by her partner

Jean van der Bijl, travelled to Westphalia in north-west Germany to meet von Laer again.

Together with *The Green Heart*, *The Water-Castle* is an imaginative mapping of that visit and the Chamberlain–von Laer relationship against the post-war hardening of Germany's borders and the wider 'zoning' of Europe. The boundaries of genre are themselves redrawn as Chamberlain attempts a fictionalisation of the self, drawing on letters from von Laer, some of which actually formed part of an early draft of the novel. Tellingly, perhaps, the book was advertised as a novel on the dust-jacket, but not on the title-page. *The Water-Castle* both verifies and contests Anthony Conran's remark that Chamberlain's work is an exercise in 'invent[ing] her own life'. An inveterate mapper of autobiography onto fiction, she 'steer[ed] her imagination between the real islands of a real outside', to the extent that her 'great act of fiction was herself', as Conran puts it.

Chamberlain's aspiration to move beyond the confines of the Welsh cultural castle leads her to explore two actual 'castles' in her novel – one imaginatively, the other literally. The first is the moated baroque *schloss* of von Laer's ancestral estate at Schlotheim, Thuringia, 'lost' now in the Russian eastern zone of Germany – a romanticised space belonging to a class-bound European past. The second is the moated manor-farm (the *Gut* or 'water-castle' of the title) to which Karl von Laer fled as a refugee after the war, and where Chamberlain visited him in the dying days of 1952.

Begun in 1953 immediately after her return from Germany, *The Water-Castle* is an eerie, ironic Cold War romance and a 'story of Europe', as a contemporary reviewer described it. Both intensely personal and profoundly public, the novel lays bare a woman's emotional hunger and creative energies in the context of the physical and emotional displacements of post-war Europe. Chamberlain emerges in this novel as a profoundly political writer, which gives the lie to the orthodox assessment of her work as untroubled by ideological debates. Mapped at the 'Obernburg' water-castle in the first section of the novel is the balkanisation of a continent. In the second section, Chamberlain's persona skis the very frontiers of the Cold War. Thus the novel's three units – 'The Water-Castle', 'Oberharz' and 'Tidal Wave' – bring the journal-writing author from the prison-sanctuary of Bardsey Island to post-war refugee-space in Westphalia; from there to the borders of a bitter Eastern bloc; then 'home' over the pitching 'salt fathoms' of the North Sea through Bardsey fantasies of death-by-water, familiar from that other (if differently) fictionalised autobiography, *Tiderace*.

'Ordinarily, I keep no sort of journal, but during those weeks on the little farm, at the water-castle, and in the Harz mountains, I recorded the events as they happened' (p. xxiii): Chamberlain casts *The Water-Castle* as the (precisely dated) 'journal' of Elizabeth Greatorex, described by Klaus von Dorn (the fictionalised von Laer) as 'the well-known English poet'. While a manuscript draft of *The Water-Castle* clearly presents Elizabeth as a *Welsh* poet and her poems as 'pure creations of North Wales', the published novel configures her as English, though the recalled first meeting with Klaus is 'in Wales' and her 'preface' identifies her as living 'on a small half-forgotten island in the Irish sea' (plainly Bardsey) where she and Antoine (the fictionalised van der Bijl) are 'forced in upon [themselves] in an often painful proximity to tides and storm and seafowl' (p. xxiii). The novel reveals the extent to which the imagination of Elizabeth Greatorex has been conditioned by Klaus's post-war letters; she inhabits a 'literary' construction of the world that is sorely tested when she is confronted by the material reality of Klaus's exile and by the obscene violence of recent history. Chamberlain has created a persona that allows her to explore not only anxieties of cultural identity and belonging, but also her fretfulness as a female artist struggling to achieve an authentic, independent and principled purchase on a world both beautiful and brutal.

Chamberlain's experimentation with the journal form, which tests the compatibility of the day-book's brief impressions and the novel's discursive expanse, points to her full acknowledgement of the extent to which her literary work is 'parasitic' (Conran's term) on 'her own biography'. Therefore, far from failing to achieve the necessary 'distance' from her subject that the novel form traditionally calls for, Chamberlain in *The Water-Castle* offers a complex autobiographical fiction, a study of a 'fantasy-haunted' and self-deluding female consciousness struggling to acknowledge unpalatable emotional truths and harsh socio-political realities.

In the first section of the novel, Elizabeth Greatorex encounters a frost-bound world of 'sad Westphalian fields' and displaced persons, identified by P. T. Hughes in a review in the *Sunday Independent* as 'postwar debris looking back in sorrow on their past glories and freedoms'. The various households to which Elizabeth is introduced are all constituted by loss. The once gracious, now damp, decaying and labyrinthine Obernburg itself – the gravitational centre of this first part – is owned by Klaus's cousin, now a political prisoner of the Russians in Siberia, where 'the former proud officer of cavalry had been put to house-painting and the digging of graves'. Chamberlain maps these Westphalian spaces in direct relation to the Siberian Gulags and the Nazi Death Camps. The Schäferhof – the 'sordid' and 'ugly' Westphalian farmstead where Klaus lives with his pregnant wife (and first cousin) Helga – is rendered sombre and oppressive by the haunting photograph of Klaus's dead first wife, Brita. (In the 'Green Heart' sequence of poems, Chamberlain's persona configures pictures of Brita as imprisoning, killing borders: 'I stand windowed in the frame of your dead love' – 'windowed' resonating here, uncannily, with 'widowed'). There is also something profoundly funereal about the 'white flowered' cyclamen chosen by Elizabeth on the day of her arrival at the Schäferhof. Nearby, Schwarzenmoor, home to Klaus's brother Johannes and his family, witnessed extreme violence when the previous inhabitants were shot dead by their Polish servants. In this deathly terrain, Klaus's Schlotheim – that dreamy ancestral house from which he was driven by the advancing Soviets – survives for the exiles as a symbol of custom and ceremony with its 'elegant proportions, its statues, its rose garden, its peacocks' (p. 14).

The Westphalian households Elizabeth inhabits in late December 1952 are not so much homes as cultural and political asylums, offering refuge (but not amnesia) to extended families, friends and dependants who yearn after a multitude of 'home[s] in the east', from which they embarked on a six-month trek along broken roads strafed by Russian machine-gun fire. Elizabeth remarks that 'They have no future such as they were born to expect'. At the Obernburg, these remnants of an anachronistic order 'recreate a little of the old grandeur of their past lives... by their winter games and hare shoots'. Elizabeth is complicit in this rehearsal of the past in a diminished present, as she yields to fantasies of being the mistress of Schlotheim – the product of a curious mix of poetic reverie and sexual yearning ('Schlotheim is part of my myth-inheritance'). Still hanging in Schlotheim, perhaps, is the self-portrait she gave Klaus all those years ago in Wales. At Schwarzenmoor, Elizabeth enquires after its fate:

> Herr von Ravenstadt went round the table, ladling the hot punch into our glasses. He was gallant to me: "The drawing you made, the self-portrait when you were a student; the one you sent to Klaus, it was a good drawing."
>
> "Where is it now? He has not still got it, has he?"
>
> "No, it was left behind in Schlotheim. The Russians have it now. Perhaps Herr Stalin put it on his bedroom wall."
>
> He laughed immoderately at his own joke. (p. 43)

It is at such moments that Chamberlain subjects her own romantic fantasies and those of her persona to ironic scrutiny. Fancies are always brought up short by cruel realities: 'In the security of his cousin's dining-room it must have been easy for Klaus to forget that next day he would have to get up in the raw darkness to pick frozen brussels sprouts for market' (p. 35).

Wounds at the Obernburg and its satellite spaces are distressingly physical. History's violence, and the division of Germany, are written on the body: Klaus himself was wounded on the Eastern front; his brother Johannes has a 'sabre scar'; Kurt Hastfer, steward of the Obernburg, whom we first see wearing 'cavalry breeches', has 'only one arm', the 'empty sleeve falling from his convulsively-twitching left shoulder'; Helga's sister's right hand has been 'hideously mutilated' by 'machine-gun fire on the way westward'; and the same woman's husband returned a 'skeleton' from another Siberian camp. The list goes on. This, then, is a landscape of fear, amputation and hurt, and it mirrors and conditions the emotional breaches of the Klaus–Elizabeth–Antoine/Karl–Brenda–Jean triangle.

The second part of *The Water-Castle* – 'Oberharz' – takes Elizabeth to the new borders that are the physical manifestations of freezing Cold War ideologies. The journal-narrative of a skiing trip to Sankt Andreasberg in the Harz Mountains, which in early 1953 was edgy frontierland divided between the British and Russian Zones, is also a nuanced analysis of the physical and psychological effects of Europe's new militarized borders. Selma Hasfter warns Elizabeth that Klaus may well be tempted to ski over the border into the lost 'green heart' of Thuringia, in an attempt to reach his ancestral Schlotheim. 1952 – the very year Chamberlain visited Germany – was the defining moment in the creation of Europe's Cold War borders. It was the year in which the 'Inner German Border' established at the end of the Second World War ceased being a relatively-easy-to-cross 'green border' and became a strict line of demarcation separating The Federal Republic of Germany in the west from the German Democratic Republic in the east. From Goslar – at this time a British garrison town – Elizabeth ascends to the Harz. The ski runs offer a sense of physical and emotional release, and yet the Harz is also a landscape of mental dislocation. One road into the village from the ski slopes, often taken by Elizabeth, leads past a 'long grey' sanatorium, gothicised by her fretful imagination until it becomes part of a 'spectral' landscape of 'demons' and 'dinosauri'. Conditioning her deepening attachment to Klaus is her sensitivity to the tense borders on which she skis, accompanied by the 'sound of firing from the Russian side of the Brocken', 'a succession of rifle shots', the barking of a patrol dog and the roar of 'Jet plane engines' in a weirdly empty sky. The emotional drama partakes of the disturbing charge with which Chamberlain invests the *verboten* spaces of these mountains. Intimate moments registered in the journal take place 'within the small zone of safety' near the border, next to 'the area of no-man's land cleared of timber' – sites of desire where Klaus can ask her 'Shall we go? We could cross the frontier at night'. 'Each day we come a little nearer to the Russians, closer to the gunfire', Elizabeth records – a statement that asks us to see emotional and physical danger as inextricably linked. She records her daily recreation and emotional unrest against the bitter geopolitical landscape, but the author's control of tone and perspective reveals that Elizabeth is still content to disavow full knowledge, both of the emotional consequences of her trip, and of the political meanings of the natural and built environment. It is in this second section that Chamberlain explores most subtly the brutality that goes into the making of national borders.

The frost of Part One of *The Water-Castle* became snow in Part Two. In the final section as Elizabeth, now back in Westphalia, 'safe in Klaus's love for another few days', prepares to leave Germany, it melts to engulfing water. Chamberlain's pen drawing at the head of the final section suggests two tide-races running in heavy spate between objects now estranged (p. 117). Sidi, Klaus's sister-in-law, is here given the most explicit political intervention in the whole novel, but the fears she articulates have been present throughout, reflecting Chamberlain's personal anxieties regarding the effects of totalitarianism and aggressive nationalism on the freedoms a female artist seeks:

What we want is internationalism, not nationalism; and true freedom for women... It is terrible, always to be in fear. I am afraid, increasingly afraid, for Inser. She is only thirteen years of age, but already, she is very tall for her years. If the Russians came, she would be noticed at once, and taken to Siberia. Perhaps this year, or maybe next year, Russia will overrun the west zone as she overran the east. The whole of Europe will become her colony. (p. 126)

It is in this atmosphere that Elizabeth now professes her love for Klaus. His response is guarded, displaced into metaphor and analogy: 'We loved one another for twenty years,' he said softly, 'but there is much water between us'; 'The wind is rising. The sea will be rough tonight'; 'Listen! the trees are roaring like the sea at high water'. *The Water-Castle* gathers to an ending that charts Elizabeth's return 'home' (that concept now radically redefined) against the inundation of the 'Big Flood' of 31 January 1953 ('the worst natural disaster to befall the British Isles during the twentieth century') when a storm-surge hit the east coast, crossed the Channel and wreaked destruction on the low coasts of Holland. Ghosting the novel's ending is Chamberlain's short story of 1947, 'The Return' – another autobiographical fiction that dramatised the fantasy of a solo crossing of the perilous sound to Bardsey Island:

> Klaus's face was printed on the night at sea.... The vessel began to pitch and shudder; she rolled sideways. I lay awake, aware of silver schools of fish; and of limp-clawed lobsters killed and brought to the surface by the submarine cataclysm; of salt fathoms, of the meaning of sea-fathoms, of fathoms deep... (p. 155)

The idiom and imagery recall *Tide-race*. In a draft of *The Water-Castle*, Elizabeth's return 'with her husband' is rendered fatal: sensationally, she drowns in Bardsey Sound 'on the crossing to their island home in a small motorboat'. The published novel ends less melodramatically, and more ambiguously, in 'storm-tossed' European waters between the Hook of Holland and Harwich. The 'in-between' geography of the ending is wholly appropriate: this is a work poised suggestively between a journal and a novel, autobiography and fiction, romance and political documentary, Welsh and European spaces, West and East, island and mainland selves. In this sense, *The Water-Castle* is both an ambitiously unconventional work and a paradigmatic 'Anglo-Welsh' text.

Damian Walford Davies

CONTENTS

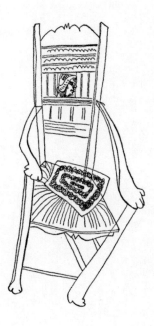

During the greater part of the year my husband and I live on a small half-forgotten island in the Irish Sea, forced in upon ourselves and a few neighbours for company, in an often painful proximity to tides and storm and seafowl.

So it is perhaps not unnatural that a visit to friends in the world outside should have assumed an exaggerated importance, or perhaps I was put to the temptation of enjoying too much sunshine. That simply is what Klaus thought, that I had been unduly impressed by 'too much sunshine', by snow and forest and high places.

Now it is all a long time over, but it seems likely to remain the most real part of my whole life.

Ordinarily, I keep no sort of journal, but during those weeks on the little farm, at the water-castle, and in the Harz mountains, I recorded the events as they happened.

Elizabeth Greatorex

AH, we count the years and make occasional cuttings of them and stop and begin again and hesitate between both. But actually everything that befalls us is of one piece, in whose correlations one thing is kith and kin with another, fashions its own birth, grows and is educated to its own needs, and we have ultimately only *to be there*, simply, fervently, as the earth is there, in harmony with the seasons, dark and light and absolutely in space, not demanding to be cradled in anything but this web of influences and powers in which the very stars seem safeguarded.

Letter to Clara Rilke

Selected letters of Rainer Maria Rilke 1902–1926 translated by R.F.C. Hull. Macmillan & Company, London 1946.

1

THE WATER-CASTLE

DECEMBER 23

AT last we are on the Schäferhof. Outside the double windows of my friends' bedroom, the year is dying over the snow-pocked Westphalian fields. A gaunt tree leans towards the raw brick house. As far as one can see, the land is flat and melancholy, with low hills forming the horizon. Farm dwellings stand apart from each other over the plain, like dolls' houses put down at random. They have steep-pitched roofs, small windows and enormous doorways, and are variously painted; white, green, and chocolate-coloured.

It is our second day at the little farm. This is the first visit I have made to Germany in the flesh, and a strange sensation arises from being confronted with the reality after one has lived here for many years in imagination. Klaus says I have written more poetry about Germany than have her native poets.

We arrived in the afternoon, my husband Antoine and I; after a long comfortless journey, from our island to London, then from Liverpool Street by way of Harwich to the Hook of Holland. The sober Dutch landscape gave us no sense of excitement, no thrill of being in a foreign land.

We had crossed the North Sea at night: on deck, in a piercingly cold breeze, we lost sense of direction, as the ship eased her way out of the harbour. The lights of other vessels were reflected in the black water. Coloured harbour lights blinked and went out, and blinked again. Further out, a bell-buoy clanged mournfully. A few people stood at the rail watching the sea slip past. A young Dutch girl came out on deck. Already, I had noticed her in the boat train. She had a plain, fresh, undistinguished face, but her hair under the deck lamps was pure shining gold. Immediately, an admirer was at her side, drawn by the sheen of her hair.

At Hook of Holland, we saw her again, while we were awaiting our turn in the passport office. We had to stand for an hour and a half in a long queue, most of the time in the street (in the darkness of early morning) under a sign that said: 'WELCOME TO HOLLAND'.

The blonde girl looked less confident now; she seemed to be having difficulty with the passport officer; and her cavalier of the boat had attached himself to two other Dutch girls. Some time later, she passed us as we stood in the corridor of the crowded train. She was smiling happily, and had a new escort. She must have been about the same age as I was when last I saw Klaus, twenty years ago.

Unlike the girl with the golden hair, I felt unsure of myself as the train ran out of Holland and into Germany.

"It is really madness," I said to myself, "to expect a man you knew twenty years ago, to be the same sort of person, still."

Klaus had written that he would be at Löhne station to meet the train, with the horse and wagon. But would he recognize me after half a lifetime of separation? Would I recognize him? All I had to go by were a few small snapshots taken the previous summer. One photograph showed his back: he was ploughing and had a powerful, still-young body. In another, he was holding his infant son in his arms. In this snapshot, he looked remarkably like my memory of him, though his face was much heavier now. He was holding his month-old son, looking down at the baby with the smile

4

I remembered. The man's strong arm held the young body, his huge hand lying protectively near the mole-like paws of the child. I had compared these snapshots with one taken of Klaus twenty years ago, when he was a law student at Königsberg. That year, he had come to spend the summer with the family of one of my school friends in my home town, where I was spending the long summer vacation.

The German landscape was flat and desolate; thin patches of snow lay on the fields; there were sparse clumps of trees at intervals. The nearer we came to Löhne, the more blanched and derelict was the landscape. We stepped down into icy mud and slush on the station platform. We had several pieces of luggage; suitcases, and small grips, and skis. Porters stood about; grey-clothed men, in peaked caps over grey faces. They refused to notice us or our belongings. There was no sign of Klaus. I thought he might be waiting beyond the ticket barrier; but he was not there, either. He might be outside in the station yard; perhaps, he could not leave the horse standing too long unattended. A wagon was coming slowly down the road. I searched the face of the wagoner as the cart drew near. His was a young face, not middle-aged, as I must expect. I was still looking for my past.

We waited in the cold booking-hall for a long time. My husband, Antoine, was moodily silent. A British officer, I suppose from the occupation forces in the caserne at Herford, was handing in suitcases at the counter of the left-luggage office. I went across and asked him if there was a possibility of our getting a taxi to take us to the Schäferhof. Schäferhof? He had never heard of the place, but it should be possible to get a taxi. In halting German he spoke to the man in the ticket hall. From behind a glass partition, the German eyed him with detachment; but he consented at last to ring for the station taxi. The driver told us there were two houses of the same name belonging to the family von Dorn; one, the larger, stood on the main Löhne-Herford road. The smaller Schäferhof was at the further side of a coppice.

"Yes, yes; that was it. You had to go through a wood to get there."

We travelled along mean roads, deeply rutted and gleaming with mud. Beyond the town the land was open, with many small farmhouses in the hedgeless fields. The taxi left the road, and we bumped along a track towards a knot of bare trees. On one of the trees a board was nailed, bearing the words: Dr. Helga von Dorn, practising veterinary surgeon. The chauffeur sounded his horn.

A massive woman great with child, in a full-skirted blue dress, clogs, and ribbed woollen stockings, a red and white kerchief over her dark hair, came out of the house door. Her head was beautiful, with a fine hooked nose and dark eyes; but her body was gross and untidy. She had the haunches of a brood mare. This, I realized, must be Klaus's second wife, of whom I knew nothing, except that she had been his wife for three years. Antoine was overcome by the vastness of the woman crossing the yard. He said aloud, "My God."

In broken English, with a generous smile, Helga greeted us. She led us through mud and rotting straw to the house. She could not understand what had gone wrong with the arrangements. Klaus had left with the wagon in good time to meet the Scandinavian Express, on which we had been expected. Now we suddenly realized that the train on which we had travelled had not been the Express; that we had missed it in the endless delay at the passport office in Holland, and that we had come by a later train; but Helga was afraid that the horse had bolted in the town.

"Does the horse often run away?"

"But yes," she replied, laughing. "Albrecht runs away with Klaus every week."

The wide house door opened into a square red-tiled hall, from the ceiling of which hung a huge paper fish. A door on the right led into the servants' kitchen and bedroom. On the left was a lavatory, and beside it, at the foot of the staircase, was the stable door. Opposite the front door was a small dining-room and beyond that, the children's nursery. At the top of the narrow stairs were two small bedrooms and an open hayloft.

After we had eaten, I went upstairs to wash, and to change my shoes for ski-boots. As I was lacing them up, I heard a commotion in the yard: then the sound of the front door opening. A man's voice shouted:

"Has she come?"

I went out onto the small landing at the turn of the stairs, up which Klaus was running to meet me.

I do not remember what we said to one another in our excitement, but I was aware of Antoine watching us from the hall below. Klaus was dressed in a green overcoat; on his head was a grey felt hat edged with green braid, and worn pulled down over one eye. He wore spectacles. The hair at his temples was almost white. His laugh was the same, his eyes were the same, so blue they gave him almost the look of a blind man, the blue of an icefall. What I was unprepared for was his warmth, his exuberant delight that I had come on a visit at last. Twenty years ago, we were shy with one another, showing no emotion. It was only after he had gone back to Germany, in his first letter, that he had shown anything of what he had come to feel for me during the days of that student summer.

He made us both sit down in the living-room while he ran out to the cart, from which he quickly returned, holding in his arms two flowerpots. Each pot contained a cyclamen; one with red flowers, the other with white. Falling on one knee with a dramatic gesture, my friend held out the two plants. "Choose," he said. "Choose the flower you like best."

Helga was not in the room, but I thought of her dark, heavy maternal aspect, and it seemed that the red blooms were more suited to her than to me. I put my white-flowered plant on a teapot-stand in the middle of the round table at which we had eaten, already thinking of how much I should like to take it back to England with me. Helga took the flame-red cyclamen upstairs into her room.

The twin babies, Gottfried and Angelika, who are just learning to walk, were brought by Anni the nursemaid, for us to see. Angelika, being more lightly built than her brother, is already able to stagger about the room. He sits, or lies on his stomach, frowning, and gazing up from blue eyes. He is like his father; the girl is like her mother.

Two old peasants live here, called affectionately, Oma and Opa. Klaus and Opa brought in the Christmas tree and took it upstairs into the bed-sitting room where Klaus and Helga sleep. With the artless enthusiasm of a boy, Klaus brought

out a box containing decorations for the tree, and the figures to go in the crib. The Child, Mary, Joseph, the beasts—cow, horse, elephant, sheep—he has modelled out of clay dug from the forest at the Obernburg, the nearby estate of his cousins, where he lived for a time after the war, with Brita his first wife. He showed me sheets of watercolours he had made. They were weakly pretty, not at all the sort of work one would expect from someone of strong personality. One watercolour, which hung in a frame over his bed, was for me more interesting than the rest. Klaus laughingly pointed it out to me.

"You did not know it was hanging here. It is of the sand dunes by the Baltic. I described them to you in a letter. You wrote a poem; I painted a picture."

There is only a single bed in my room, so Antoine has to sleep out at a neighbouring farm, with a peasant family. The farmer, whom they call Uncle Fritz, was kind and helpful to Klaus and Helga when they first came to live at the Schäferhof.

Oma does the cooking and milking; Opa, who is a tall, evil-looking old man, chops the wood, works in the fields, and takes the milk churns to the road each morning. Anni the nursemaid is very young, not more than sixteen; she is typically German, blonde and pretty.

The hall stinks of pig food and brussels sprouts. There is a smell from the stable as well, but most overpowering of all is the stench from the lavatory.

IT is the night of Christmas Eve. I am writing this in bed. At five o'clock this evening, we went to church in a small village on the road to Herford. It was pitch-dark, cold and raining, as the four of us set out in the wagon behind the horse Albrecht. Klaus and Helga were on the driving seat; Antoine and I sat behind in basket chairs taken from the living-room. Klaus had insisted on muffling us in topcoats over our own coats, and he had put rugs over our knees. Helga held a small lantern at the side of the cart as a warning to motorists. We went downhill for a long way, with the brake on, crossed a hollow-sounding bridge over an invisible river, and soon after, reached the space before the church. We were late for the service; they were singing a hymn.

"It is not a beautiful or a remarkable church," Helga had explained. "But it is convenient for us, and we like it because we were married here."

Klaus tied Albrecht to a tree outside the door, and we went inside. The church was packed. Heads turned to stare as we came in: we stood near the wall. Each of us was handed a paper on which was printed the order of the service. The building was lit simply by the candles on the two tall Christmas trees by the altar. I could imagine how Antoine, as a Roman Catholic, must have been repelled by the stark Lutheran service. For me it was different; it was a familiar experience of my soul, like all else happening so suddenly, threatening to overcome my usual calm. These candled fir trees were synonymous with those translated from Klaus's description in a letter, to form an image in one

of my first poems. Having made the poem out of his experience, I now so late shared his experience and found the poem true. I felt myself to be going backwards in time.

I was aware of his tall presence where he stood some way behind me with his wife.

Klaus's elder brother Johannes and his wife Sidi came this evening with Christmas gifts for the twins. Johannes looks much older than Klaus, though he is actually only two years his senior. He has a kindly wrinkled face, sensuous lips, a sabre scar, and grey hair. I can imagine him in uniform, a typical Prussian officer; though, in reality, he never served in the army. He does not speak English, but Sidi, his wife, does. She has Turkish, English, and German blood. She is sallow, dark-haired, with snapping eyes, and a thin-lipped mouth, but she is lively, and I should think, highly intelligent and restless. She has invited us to visit them after Christmas on their big farm Schwarzenmoor, which lies the other side of Herford.

Tonight, Klaus showed me many photographs taken during the German invasion of Russia. At first, it was strange to look at pictures of 'the other side', of 'the enemy'; gradually, one grows used to it. Snow, horses, mud, thatched huts, poverty; that is the impression given by the photographs. The slight squint in his right eye became more noticeable as he stared into the past.

We were upstairs in Helga's room, where the tree with its candles and tinsel and bonbons stood, sheltering the heavy clay figures in the crib. The twin babies were brought up by Anni, and presented with their new toys. Gottfried sat on the floor, staring with round eyes at the candlelight; his sister, who is much smaller, and quicker in her reactions, trotted about the floor, poking her hands into the gift boxes. The old peasants came upstairs for a short time, to hear Klaus read aloud from the Bible. They were awed and shy, and seemed glad to escape to their own quarters.

Before dinner, the old Oma came to me with a bottle of schnapps. It was the first time I had ever tasted such strong spirit. Because I was hungry, it made me feel tipsy and sick. I came to bed as early as I could. When I looked in the mirror a few minutes ago, my face surprised me by its horrible grey-white colour.

It is sad to have to kiss Antoine good night on the doorstep, to lock the door after him as he walks off into what is to me still an unknown landscape.

The bed is hard and uncomfortable and the thick feather eiderdown nearly stifles me.

I am reading Hemingway's *Old Man And The Sea*, a lovely book, moving quietly and surely page after page. It makes me think of the island in summertime. To my surprise, Antoine for all his expert interest in fishing was bored by the tale. In small, as in important things, we seem to be growing ever further apart.

Tomorrow is Christmas Day.

Not for the first time, I find myself wondering what has happened to Brita, Klaus's first wife, to whom he must have been married about ten years. There was a long pause in Klaus's letters about four years ago. Then, without any explanation, he sent me the formal announcement of his marriage to Helga. That was three years ago. I have no idea of what can have happened, whether Brita is divorced or dead.

In Klaus's and Helga's bedroom is a photograph of a girl's head in profile. It must be Brita.

The wind whistles through the door of the hayloft which is next to my room.

CHRISTMAS DAY

THE babies are growing accustomed to our faces: now they no longer look alarmed when either of us comes into the room. Gottfried, who is like his father in appearance, will probably have the same easily-silenced temperament. Angelika has the colouring of hair and eyes and the wide-mouthed smile of her mother. The children sit with us at breakfast, putting their sticky hands into everything on the table. According to Helga, Klaus had eyes only for his son, when the twins were born.

The house is sordid: a miserable shivering mongrel called Yula messes wherever she pleases, in the living-room or in the hall, and a ginger and white cat is always in the room where we eat. A sickly smell of babies fills the air. A few paintings, mostly Klaus's work, have been hung about the house. There is a self-portrait, and two landscapes, one showing two large goat-like sheep, the other, turkeys. Helga pointed out a watercolour of sunflowers hanging above the big cupboard in the hall.

"That was painted by an artist," she explained. "By a friend of Klaus. You will meet her when you go to the Obernburg."

It is pleasant to have the luxury of an hour's siesta each afternoon. Helga and Klaus rest in their room: Antoine and I lie head to feet on my bed.

There is a small wood-burning stove in Helga's room. It is kept alight continuously at this time of year, so that the small low-ceilinged room is gloriously warm. On the wireless cabinet are two photographs. One is of a young man with a sabre-scar on his face; this is one of Helga's brothers, killed in the war. The other photograph is of Brita.

The warmth of the stove brings out the fragrance of the Christmas fir tree. It was cut in the forest of the Obernburg, where we are to go the day after tomorrow for a hare shoot. This evening we have been singing carols round the lighted tree, with Antoine accompanying us on Helga's harmonica. Afterwards, Klaus showed us old albums of snapshots taken at his former home, the castle Schlotheim now in Russian hands. What a contrast there is between this ugly Westphalian farm and the baroque schloss with its elegant proportions, its statues, its rose garden, its peacocks! One picture showed a young girl in a white dress seated on a flight of stone steps with a dog at her feet. Her face was shadowed in a falling curtain of dark hair.

Helga was downstairs, when Klaus said in a painful half-strangled voice:

"That is Brita."

Did she die, or has she gone away to another part of Germany, or to America? Antoine was present in the room, so I did not ask for an explanation. All I know is that they were together until four years ago, after being reunited at the end of the war. They had fled from the east into the western zone, and had

14

lived for some time in the Obernburg. Helga's old nurse, who was with her family for many years, is to come here for the lying-in, and to look after the twins for the rest of the winter.

They go to bed early here even on Christmas Night because they have to get up in the dark, at about five o'clock in the morning. The house is full of strange faces. In the kitchen, Opa and Oma entertain their children: both the old ones have grown-up families by different mates. They too are refugees from East Prussia, and they only married about three years ago. Oma looks tired and sad, with the blind gaze of the very old. Dark glasses hide her husband's eyes, so that one has no idea whether he has poor sight or good. He wears a greasy peaked peasant cap. One of his daughters is in the house over the holiday: she is a young woman of terrifying aspect. She may well have been a wardress in a prison camp, for she is a giant with a brutal face. Wearing dark trousers under a wide blue skirt, she sits at the kitchen table before a small mirror, endlessly brushing her coarse hair. Several times, I have tried to make her smile, with no result. As soon as she sees me, her scowl becomes more intense. She unnerves me so much that I can no longer force myself to go into the kitchen if I think she is likely to be there. It is a relief to know that Helga and Klaus view her with the same horror. She works in one of the many cigar factories near Herford. Judging by the uproar, there must have been a crowd of peasants in the kitchen tonight. Helga told me that one of Oma's sons was there; a worker on the local railway. He has an unpleasant habit of coming to the farm at night, and trying the door. If he finds it has been left unlocked, he comes inside to steal small objects, such as teaspoons or knives or a plate. Oma herself warned her employers of his bad habits.

Helga is so heavy with child that she feels obliged to rest every evening, her fingers constantly busy in a box of chocolates. When she is in a gracious mood, she can be charming; she tries hard to entertain us, but keeps our conversation on the lightest level. I cannot feel close to her as I do to Klaus. With him it is quite another matter: we are so attuned that we instinctively avoid speaking or even looking at one another when Helga or Antoine is in the room. How is it possible that we should have remained the same to one another after so many years?

Today, I discovered that Klaus and Helga are first cousins; though they met for the first time only a few months before they were married. Helga had been staying with her cousin Sophie at the Obernburg on the eve of her departure for South Africa where she hoped to practise as a veterinary surgeon. She had already bought her ticket, and her trunks were packed. On a sudden impulse, Klaus asked her to be his wife.

"So I did not get to South Africa," she told me, with a strange smile. Klaus calls it "The Gioconda smile".

Klaus's mother and stepfather are spending the holiday with Johannes and Sidi at their farm Schwarzenmoor. On the day we visit there, we hope to discuss, with the assembled family, plans for a ski-trip into the mountains. Two places have been suggested. Winterberg which is only a few hours distant, and Sankt Andreasberg in the Oberharz. We have asked Klaus and Helga to come with us. Helga cannot come because of her pregnancy (she expects her baby sometime in March), but Klaus will try to get away for a week at the end of our time in the mountains.

Infinite care will be necessary to carry me through the coming weeks. The need for tact became obvious at once, when Klaus first ran up the stairs to greet me on my arrival, when he gave me the pot of cyclamen.

Helga said to me yesterday:

"You have known Klaus for twenty years. I have only known him for three."

How I wish that Helga and I could be candid with one another; but she never relaxes her party manners with me. I came to Germany prepared to like her. Now, by a conversation we have just had together, my heart is estranged from her; I am on my guard. She was preparing to rest in her room after lunch; with what I took to be gentle kindness, she called me in for a little conversation. She immediately began to criticize Klaus, naming a list of petty annoyances, mostly to do with the horse and cart. She accused him of having careless accidents; for instance, in the autumn, the cart had been overturned and damaged. Klaus had gone off for a week's holiday on the Ostsee, leaving her to have the cart repaired. When he came back, he made no mention of the cart's having been mended.

She smiled, and dismissed me, leaving these small poison drops to infect my ears.

"We have had a nice little talk, and we must both rest. It is good to know you for a friend, and Antoine and Klaus get on so well together."

I was glad to escape to my room, where I spent an hour reading *The Old Man And The Sea*.

Before going to bed, Helga suggested a stroll through the wood, in order that we should sleep better. It was very dark, with neither moon nor stars. We stumbled along the cart ruts, on the road skirting the wood, the side furthest from the Schäferhof. Dogs barked at us from nearby farms. Helga stumbled so badly in the furrowed ground, that I took her arm. We walked together for a while; then she called out to the men, who were walking ahead:

"It is stupid for the women to walk together, and the men together. We will change over."

Klaus, without speaking, linked his arm in hers, and I placed my hand on Antoine's arm; there was no response from him. Entering the wood from the high-road, we walked two by two under the black trees. I sensed; how, it is impossible to say, that Klaus wanted to walk with me.

DECEMBER 26

WE found ourselves caught up this morning in an excitement over the hare shoot at the Obernburg, the water-castle of Klaus's cousins. To set out in the wagon causes a commotion even among the turkeys. Sleigh bells were spoken of, a flute was produced, knives flashed, chains and ropes were called for, until at last we declared ourselves to be ready. Albrecht the horse is liable to bolt at any time and for no good reason. He is the most unpredictable, addle-minded horse imaginable. Obernburg being almost an hour's drive away, we had to start after an early breakfast. While we were getting ready, the old peasants fussed round us, muttering dark warnings. They expect disaster to fall on anyone who trusts himself to such a horse. We squeezed ourselves into extra overcoats, farm-smelling and wolfish-furred, for there is a bitter frost and snow on the ground. The two rickety basket chairs with cushions were placed opposite one another in the body of the cart for Antoine and me to sit on. Helga insisted upon sitting beside her husband on the driving seat though it must have caused her discomfort. She refuses to stay quietly at home even so late in her pregnancy, but her condition makes her irritable and nervous, particularly when she rides behind Albrecht.

"He is a good horse to ride," she told me. "But in the cart he is dangerous."

I studied their backs, Klaus's and Helga's, as they sat square and heavy before us. They are alike in build but unlike in colouring and features and temperament. Klaus crouches owlishly over the reins, but Helga sits upright, looking with detachment at the countryside. Those we passed in the road stared at us as if they had never seen such extraordinary types before in their lives.

As it approaches the Obernburg, the road runs under an avenue of cherry trees, turns uphill, and skirts the farm buildings of the estate. So this was the reality behind the dream, the reality behind the poem of the ice-covered moat round the sleeping castle. It is exactly as it was in my imagination. My mental picture had been a curious one though, for all it had been crystal-clear, showing the pale-coloured façade from the end of the wall to the bridge over the moat, on the left side. There had been nothing of the other half of the façade. The focus of the image had been the dark windows at the furthest end of the wall above the stagnant water.

The iron cart wheels set up a tumbril-din on the cobbled bridge. We clattered into the inner courtyard under a wide stone archway over which was carved a coat-of-arms and the name of Klaus's cousin.

A house-entrance was on either side of the arch, kitchen doors were ajar within the yard, and piggeries formed the back wall of the square within the courtyard. We went in at the right-hand private door, peeled off our outer garments, throwing them together onto a chair in the stone-flagged hall, and went up and down stairs and along so many corridors that I lost my sense of direction. As we passed a certain door, Helga said: "That is where Klaus's mother and father live, but they are away at present, staying on the farm of Klaus's brother Johannes."

We crossed the dark and solemn study of Sophie von Dorn, Klaus's and Helga's cousin, until having passed through a long hall lit by tall uncurtained windows and furnished with elegant chairs and rugs, we reached the Hastfers' apartment. So, it was still possible, after two world-convulsing wars! A group of sportsmen were seated at an elaborate breakfast in the high-ceilinged room. The atmosphere was oppressively warm, and damp as a glasshouse. On an iron stove a bubbling pan was sending out steam which travelled along the ceiling to be condensed on the wall between the windows. Pools of water had formed on the floor. One or two of the sportsmen were in shooting jackets, while others were wearing long green full-skirted coats. Three boys of about ten years of age, in berets and grey or green hunting jackets and knickerbockers,

raised, was taking aim at an imaginary bird in a far corner of the room.

"He wanted me to put the angel on a rope and pulley so that he could draw it down to his gift table. He does not like it to be fixed up there out of reach, because he feels it is his own particular angel."

Of the men seated at the table, besides Kurt Hastfer and Klaus and Johannes, there were two young Westphalian landowners, brothers, and a tall thin young man with small eyes, who watched us with a cynical air. Klaus was entirely at home here, far more than in his own house. He was a great favourite with these children. They gathered round him, teasing and attracting attention, with cries of: "Uncle Klaus, Uncle Klaus, look at me."

Their attitude to Helga was severely different. They left her alone as if she had been a stranger of whom they stood in awe, while she was constrained with everyone as if she had been a visitor instead of being of the family and one who since childhood had been a constant visitor to the Obernburg. Perhaps she felt the ghost of Brita too strong for her.

On five gift tables the family presents were displayed; toys for the children, and silk stockings, an evening bag, handkerchiefs and books for the grown-ups. On another table stood eleven pots each holding a pruned geranium. The sun made transparent the tender stems on which furry pink bracts were visible.

Antoine and I would have liked to go out into the forest, but Helga explained to us that we must stay behind, and go walking with her in the garden.

23

"I will show you the children's play-house," she said, with her grande dame air. "Afterwards, we are to take lunch with my cousin, and this afternoon we can go out with the guns, if you wish."

Their hunger satisfied, the huntsmen gathered on the bridge over the moat whose ice-glazed waters held in its crust the blackened remains of a raft. Weeping birches hung almost to the surface of the ice. Servants ran back and fore over the cobblestones of the yard. A coachman in a smart trap behind a black thoroughbred set off up the road. The green-coated gentlemen, one of whom carried a shining horn at his back, moved away into the darkness of the forest. Seeing Klaus among his family and friends made me feel distant from him, more distant than when we were physically hundreds of miles apart. He was swallowed up as if it would be for ever under the dark trees, followed by a straggle of beaters, old men and young boys.

Helga said: "Come, I will show you where I played as a child. In summertime, it is a place of roses."

She was trying to create an illusion, to build comfort out of the wintry derelict garden. From despair at her own heaviness, her weighed-down maternity, she conjured her childhood-self that had run among rose bushes and had played in a stone pavilion now lying in fragments on the frozen grass. The child she had been leapt from her eyes, to run lightly before us past bushes of phantom blossom into the balsam odours of the forest.

"In summertime," she repeated, "it is a place of roses. They hang down the walls and climb the bridges over the water. Roses... roses..."

Sighing, she turned to Antoine, murmuring: "My cousin does not permit that you should go out this morning with the guns, but after lunch we shall go to meet them when they come out of the woods. Then you can follow the shoot during the afternoon."

She sighed again, this time deeply.

"In my home in the east, we arranged these things better. Many more neighbours came for the sport. A hundred hares would be laid out at dusk in the courtyard. Hampers of food and drink were taken into the fields to refresh the shooting party. My father had a gift for the gaieties of life."

Recollecting herself, she glanced up and away to a black corner at the lower edge of the trees.

"He is buried over there in the family cemetery."

"Your mother," I asked. "Is she still alive?"

"Yes, she lived here for a time after the war. Now she lives in Bavaria. My sister lives here at the Obernburg with her husband and son. We are to take coffee with her this afternoon. Come!" she urged with a sudden change of mood. "I must show you the children's garden house where I used to play with my dolls."

We crossed the road and came to a rough patch of land adjoining the kitchen gardens and the greenhouses. The children's house was a full-sized cottage with half-timbered walls, a steeply-pitched roof, a tall chimney, and shutters to the unglazed windows. There was a miniature moat round it in imitation of the castle, and plank bridges spanned the ditch. Inside was an open fireplace and a long trestle table for parties. On the walls Selma and Vivica had painted murals of fairy-tale characters, Red Riding Hood, the wolf, Hansel and Gretel and the old witch, angels and mythical animals. Helga pointed out the figures to us, as though they held no interest for her, but were part of her duty as hostess.

Lunch was served in Sophie's apartment, not in the principal room giving onto the garden, but in a smaller room with long windows overlooking the courtyard. Sophie von Dorn did not eat with us. She and Selma Hastfer had gone out with the guns for the whole day. A subtly-smiling, quiet little woman, her secretary-companion, deputized for her at the head of the table. Helga and the secretary were civil to one another with a forced politeness as if they knew too much about one another and did not like what they knew.

Helga had a good appetite and ate with impatient haste. She would not sit at table a moment longer than was necessary. Here at the Obernburg her hand hovered over the bell to summon the maid almost before the rest of us were halfway through a course.

Glancing up at the window, I saw a small car coming into the yard. A man got out of the driving seat, carrying a white cardboard box.

"Ah, my brother-in-law," Helga laughed. "Look at his car! Isn't it like a cigar box? He has bought cakes for our tea this afternoon."

The day was mercilessly cold. The three of us, Antoine, Helga, and I walked up a long hill in hope of coming upon the shooting party. It was some time before we heard the guns. There was a faraway sound of firing from the forest near the summit of the road. The black horse and trap came briskly up behind us.

26

"Would it not be more comfortable for you to sit in the trap?" I asked Helga.

The coachman was halted, and we climbed up to sit on the cold leather-padded seats, with two dead hares at our feet.

A roe deer, disturbed by the invasion of its territory, ran out of cover and galloped across the open fields towards the sheltering valley. Nervously, the horse pricked its ears at the stuttering of the guns. Two men riding horses passed us on their way to plough out frozen turnips in the high fields. These horses, and the fine thoroughbred behind which we sat, had been among those brought on the trek from the east, Helga told me. The horses had been on the roads for six months at a stretch, carrying refugees, furniture, books, china, and plate.

The horn! The horn! A hare on long-springing legs ran up the ploughed field, followed by a straggle of beaters. A man appeared in front of a tree. It was Klaus, with a gun at his shoulder. He fired, but missed the hare.

Antoine threw up his arms, shouting exultantly:

"Oh, bad luck, bad shot."

The hare ran on, into the protection of the forest. As more and more sportsmen appeared at the edge of the trees, Helga remarked, looking back over her shoulder:

"There is Klaus with his friend."

Selma and Klaus had walked out onto the open land. Their heads were thrown back in laughter. I found myself shivering in the great cold.

Beaters grasping sticks in their hands, came in a line towards us, while at the top of the field, in a bare space

27

between two areas of cultivated land, Sophie waited with schnapps and sandwiches. Antoine and I were now told we might follow the guns. Helga said she was too tired to stay out any longer, and would return to the castle to take a rest in her cousin's room.

Antoine went down the road with Kurt Hastfer, but before they went, Kurt told me to stand behind a tree, well away from the firing, and near the younger of the two brothers whom we had met at breakfast, the one who carried the horn. With him was the tall young man with the mocking eyes. The men turned to me and began to bewail the passing of the big estates. Telling me that he had been a prisoner in Siberia, the thin young man spoke with bitterness.

"There are thousands and thousands of Germans still imprisoned in Russia. Do you know that the man who owns this estate is still there?" he asked.

"Yes, I know."

He also had lost his lands in the east and had sought refuge in Westphalia. He had married a woman of property and so had become a landowner once more.

"The way things are going, we shall lose everything again," he grumbled. "The government will try to break up the large properties into smallholdings."

His mood changing, he turned a laughing face down to me, and said with a gleam in his small eyes:

"You are staying with Klaus on his little farm? It is a very small property, is it not? But then, he will be the lucky one in the end, no doubt, for the government cannot take anything more away from him. He has just enough land from which to make a living."

The plump young man fingered his horn, waiting for a signal from Kurt Hastfer.

"This horn," he said, touching it with loving fingers, "is one of the few romantic things left to us."

From far down the road, Kurt raised his hat high in the air as a signal. Behind me, the young man, with an elegant flourish, blew a few evocative notes, and the beaters strung out across the field, making for a small quarry. They drew a blank there, and moved back into the woods.

Having been told to stand behind the man with the horn, I remained where I was, while Antoine went away with a party including Peter Christian and Johannes's son. As I stood there idly, growing more and more cold, I wondered where Klaus had gone to. It was a long time since I had last seen him.

Sticks were being beaten in the undergrowth. In front of us was a small clearing in the trees. We were looking towards this spot, expecting to see the beaters pass there, when a hare with bulging eyes ran straight towards us out of the wood. The hornblower swung round, letting off both barrels as if through my head.

Instinctively, I leapt behind him as he swung. The hare stopped a few yards beyond us, fell sideways, and kicked in the death agony. The young man, insolently correct, bowed to me as he doffed his feathered hat.

"Excuse me, excuse me."

Kurt appeared on the path, his black eyes impressively serious. The two men raised their hats to one another and bowed with ceremony. They shook hands while Kurt offered his congratulations.

From time to time, I saw in gaps between the trees the coachman picking up dead hares.

On a desolate open field near a flour-mill, I re-encountered the tall man who had told me of his imprisonment in Russia.

"Truly, your husband is a master of shooting."

"Why do you say that?"

"He told me of how, when he is at home, he is never without a gun. Kurt Hastfer, he also is a master," he added, pointing across the field to where Kurt was walking.

"How is it possible for him to shoot with only one arm?"

"In a moment you will see, he replied. "I think they will drive a hare from below, and you will understand."

A few minutes later, a hare did bound across in the direction of the railway line. Kurt ran to an earth bank, threw himself across it with his gun tucked under his empty sleeve, and fired with his left hand. The hare dropped dead.

"You see," said my companion. "He is a master, like your husband."

It was difficult to know how much malice lay behind his light mockery. He went on: "There are two sorts of hare. One sort prefers windswept shelterless plough land, the other loves to lie secretly in the woods."

The hunt moved past the mill, along the railway track and under a bridge. Klaus and Antoine were nowhere to be seen. I had become caught up in a rabble of beaters; half-grown children with sleek blond heads, rough old men, and youths in caps and ill-fitting suits. The bridge, they told me, was mined, but for what reason was not explained. As they walked under the bridge, the boys beat on the walls and shouted, setting up a sickening and brutal echo in the iron girders.

Evening was setting in over the flat fields. We passed a group of peasants' houses and at length arrived at the quiet-flowing waters of the Werre. The hunt was over, and the whole party drew together on the river bank. To see Klaus again after the few hours of separation filled me with a singular sensation, disappointment that he had shown no interest in me during the day, and a sudden happiness, a sense of homecoming, as I walked to where he stood talking with Johannes. Even then, he barely seemed to notice, turning towards me a blind face. He is now a man of forty, but he can look almost as young as when I knew him first as a student. At other times, he looks much older than his years. This was one of those 'old' times. Last evening he was young, full of warm eagerness and enthusiasm, asking me about my life and work, filling my lap and cluttering the sofa with sheets of paper covered with watercolours painted in the Bavarian mountains.

Johannes's boy, carrying a dead sparrow-hawk, came towards me, surrounded by young companions. In small idle groups we drifted homewards. Cold and hungry, we regained the castle at dusk. Before going into the courtyard, I leaned on the stone parapet of the bridge, and lost myself in the dream of the castle and the moat. The building was long and low and water-stained at its foundations, with faded yellow-ochre walls to which wooden trellises had been affixed for the training of roses. Near me, at this side of the moat, a coal tit was footprinting the white boughs of a willow whose trailing hair had been caught in the ice.

How strange! The same weather, the same season of the year in this real Obernberg of solid stone, where a real clock records time in the tower over the archway. Klaus appearing suddenly beside me, broke into my abstraction. Glancing up into the branches of the trees, he said:

"At Schlotheim in the winter, peacocks used to roost in the trees. I liked to watch them with their tails hanging down from the branches on moonlit lights."

In a low voice he continued, pointing towards the end of the façade of the castle, on the left of the archway:

"Those two windows at the end were the rooms where Brita and I lived."

I walked forward, and he looked round him like a blind man whose white wand has been snatched away.

This was my proof, the reason why, in my mental image, I had seen only half the façade. The bridge, the frozen waters, the windows had been there. They were all I had needed. The link between Klaus and myself had been so strong that I had been almost unconsciously living in him and through him these many years. The windows he had pointed out were the dead windows of locked rooms. Here was the opportunity to ask a question about his past, about Brita, but I could not bring myself to do so, because Antoine was on his way over to us.

"Don't you want to go in?" he demanded impatiently. "I am dying of cold."

Under the archway the coachman stood with a bucket of warm water and a scrubbing brush to clean our boots.

Helga was waiting at the back door. At the sight of his wife, Klaus abruptly left us, without a word or a glance in her direction, and went indoors at the opposite side of the yard. We followed Helga, past a row of hares laid out neatly on the cobblestones, through the kitchen quarters, and upstairs to take tea with her sister. On the staircase before us ran Sophie, who smiled back at us from bright, excited eyes. Her naturally florid cheeks were flushed. She had changed from the rough tweeds she had worn in the fields into a stiff black silk frock with a full skirt, silk stockings and black shoes. She was carrying with triumphant vigour a dish holding a pie covered with elaborate pastry. She disappeared into the room above. I heard the door open on a gust of masculine laughter.

Helga's sister was barely to be seen, so dark was her apartment. She was a tall emaciated woman with a crumpled face. She gave me her left hand as Kurt had done, with a cold, "How do you do".

I glanced down at her right hand and saw that it was hideously mutilated.

The room was long and narrow and poorly furnished; the dingy walls were covered with photographs and framed drawings. A small Christmas tree stood in the corner. The husband came in. He was tall and cadaverous, with thin lips and pointed teeth, so that I was put in mind of an aristocratic rat. He wore the green jacket and breeches of a sportsman, and must have been at the shoot, though I had not noticed him.

"My brother-in-law," said Helga, "was a prisoner of war in Siberia. Poor man, he was a skeleton when he returned to us. He is a Latin scholar, and has no English"

The table was laden with different kinds of cake. We had

begun to eat, when Klaus's head appeared round the edge of the door.

"Ah, you are there," he said to me.

"Come in," Helga's sister called out.

"No, I cannot stay. I only came to see whether they had found you." He rushed away, as if pursued.

Helga, who had looked strained while Klaus was in the room, now recovered her party spirits and became livelier than I had yet seen her, addressing most of her remarks to her brother-in-law for whom she obviously had a great fondness. The sisters showed little interest in one another. With her twisted hand holding a cigarette, the elder sister smoked steadily, but the nervous tension on her face never relaxed. She had the air of a martyr, a martyr determined that others should recognize her suffering.

Helga said in a loud voice: "At the height of the trek from the east, the Obernburg housed ninety-five people, members of our family, friends, and peasants. Even now, there are still twenty-eight people living here."

After coffee, I wandered through unlighted corridors until having completely lost my way among so many rooms and passages and hearing voices behind one of the doors, I tapped and entered. Through dense tobacco smoke I could see in the hazy light of candles, the huntsmen and Sophie and Selma seated at the dinner table. So loud was their talk and laughter that they did not hear or see me. They were scarcely to be distinguished through the smoke of cigarettes and cigars. I felt like a child who, having been sent to bed, secretly descends the stairs to peep at the grown-ups. How secure they seemed in their traditional way of life. This part

34

of the house had seen no change; the furniture and rare china, the family portraits, were in the positions they had occupied for generations. In the security of his cousin's dining-room it must have been easy for Klaus to forget that next day he would have to get up in the raw darkness to pick frozen brussels sprouts for market. The diners did not notice me, so, shutting the door quietly, I groped my way until I found my way back to the apartment of Helga's sister.

"We are to spend the evening with the Hastfers," said Helga. "Selma will not be there yet, but we can sit in her room."

She seemed to be upset that we as her guests had not been invited to join the huntsmen at dinner.

"It would have been interesting for you to have met our friends."

The children and the grandmother were waiting for us. Helga took us through the room with the Christmas tree and the flying angel, through a second room with murals by Selma (kingfishers and storks), a room part-bedroom, part-dining-room. A third room had a corner curtained off by a hanging carpet. Behind the carpet was a tall mirror and a dressing table and wash-stand.

Vivica displayed the same feverish excitement as she had shown in the morning. She brought out the family treasure, an illuminated mediaeval missal wrapped in a flame-coloured silk handkerchief.

"Mammi brought this all the way from our home," she said. "Now I will show you the book with pictures from Sankt Andreasberg. My mammi made them. Will you go to ski in Sankt Andreasberg?"

She put her mother's day-book into my hands, a diary made up of prose descriptions and light-hearted drawings, and photographs of figures modelled out of snow. She explained that in February it was the custom to hold a competition in Andreasberg for the best snow-creation. Gazing at me with shining eyes, the child said: "There are fairy-tale woods in the Harz mountains. Mammi told me about them."

On a desk in the corner of the room there was a small photograph in an oval silver frame. This I supposed was another picture of Brita. Why, since her face is everywhere, is so little mention made of her?

Selma came in, looking radiant, accompanied by Klaus and Kurt. Selma took me by the hand and led me to a curiously carved chair in the middle of the room.

"Please to sit here," she commanded. "This is the seat of honour, the chair of my grandmother, who is still alive in Holstein. She came with us on the trek, and sat always on this chair in the tractor."

"These carpets," she went on, pointing to the wall and the floor, "they formed the walls of our house on the journey. We were six months on the roads, and many of us died, particularly the young children and the very old people."

Klaus came for us, impatient now to be gone, so we struggled into our heavy coats, and went to the farm buildings where Albrecht was stabled. He was in a warm barn full of sheep and goats.

When we alighted from the cart at the door of the Schäferhof we found the house locked and in darkness.

"Oma is nervous," explained Helga, rattling the door handle.

At last, the old woman heard us, and turned the key and let down the chain, but she was careful not to let us see her. She disappeared quickly into her own quarters.

A sense of complete security went through me as I lay awake in bed, an extraordinary realization that as long as I was near Klaus, I was safe. With him, I was not in a foreign land, but at home. How long it had taken me to realize this truth. It would soon be daylight, when he would kiss my hand and say that the morning was fair. For him, so close to the natural world, every dawn is surely full of wonder.

DECEMBER 27

TODAY we decided to visit Johannes and his family at their farm, Schwarzenmoor. The twins were again left in the care of Anni and the old people. Jula the shivering little dog went with us, scouting along the road and chasing hares in the fields. She had no sense of danger on the roads. It became so nerve-racking to watch her narrow escapes from under the wheels of cars and lorries that at last she was caught and put for safety into Helga's arms.

The basket chair made it fairly comfortable to sit in the cart, except when the wheel ran, as it frequently did, into a deep rut. Then the chair slid about the floor, threatening to upset the balance. It is evident that Klaus and his wife are considered eccentric by their neighbours. On this day, it was especially noticeable. The local peasants were out in their best clothes; it was Sunday afternoon. Their faces wore expressions of incredulity as we passed them. I realized then that the von Dorns were the only people I had seen paying a visit in a farm wagon.

"These folk think we are mad," I called out to Klaus.

"Oh yes, they are so afraid of their horses, and they beat them so, that they are afraid to sit in their carts, and must always walk safely on the ground."

The mad count and his friends from abroad!

Schwarzenmoor is about two miles distant from the town of Kahlberg, and it lies at the other side of the low hills that form our horizon. Beyond Herford, whilst going up the Stiftberg past the Helga Schule, Klaus told me of how at a certain period of the war, when things were going badly for the German invasion forces, the ski-troops were ordered to make bonfires of their equipment.

He said: "Can you imagine it? Mountains of skis and ski sticks going up in smoke."

On the highest point of the road lay a thin covering of frozen snow. Antoine, Klaus and I walked up the hill through the snowy area, while Helga came up slowly behind us in the wagon.

Johannes's farmhouse lies in a hollow below a road cut through a wood of tall silent trees. It is a typical farmstead of the province, with painted Gothic inscriptions forming a decoration over the immense double doors. Contained within the horse-yard are the animals, the farm machinery, the tractor and car.

We were received by Johannes and Sidi and two of their children, the elder ones, Justi and Inser. Justi I remembered as being the boy with the dead hawk, and Inser had been the girl with Medusa-hair, asleep beside the stove at the Obernburg.

"She thinks of nothing but horses," said her mother.

"Yesterday, Johannes found her in the field eating a turnip. She took a bite, then the horse took a piece. One day, without doubt, we shall find her bedded down in the stables."

A handsome young man was in the room. It was hard to know whether he was of the family or a guest, but he looked shy and unhappy and spoke to no one. When Helga came in some time after the rest of us, he looked at her swollen and heavy body under the blue cotton frock with shocked amazement. From the way he looked at Helga, it would seem that he is not of the family.

She was exhausted after the long drive, and now rested on a stiff Biedemayer settee, looking even less assured than she had done at the Obernburg. She has some quality that makes people keep away from her, especially children. A tall elderly woman of an impressive dignity came into the room. It was with an aloof but not unfriendly air that she sat in a high-backed chair at the head of the table. She was tired and withdrawn as if remembering the past.

"My mother-in-law," said Sidi.

The mother of Klaus and Johannes came out of her reverie.

"Helga," she said, "you look worn out. Go upstairs and rest for a few hours."

I think that Helga, though she is ill at ease with her relations, hates to feel left out of anything, but her mother-in-law at last coaxed her to give in to the lassitude that made her drag her feet like an old woman. Klaus left his mother to go with her, to see that she made herself comfortable. He neither speaks to her nor looks at her in public.

We had already sat down for afternoon coffee when Herr von Ravenstadt, Klaus's stepfather, a woman guest, and a charming child, came into the room. The child Kornelius is Sidi's younger son. His head is extraordinarily beautiful, small and fragile, the back of the skull perfectly formed. He has brilliantly dark eyes, rose-red cheeks, and hair worn long like a page's with a fringe across the brow. He was wearing under a hooded grey cloak a dark-blue mediaeval-style blouse with red embroidery.

Herr von Ravenstadt, a lively, young-old man with a duelling scar on his cheek, spoke of the old days when Klaus had been in Wales.

"Klaus has translated your poems for me," he said.

Inser, who had been too restless to sit down at table, now reappeared wearing her almost grown-up confirmation suit. She prowled like a newly-caged animal about the room, striding with long steps across the floor, arms held stiffly to her sides, the palms turned inward. Behind her head, the dove-coloured sky was thick with about-to-fall snow. Coquettish and shy, a child and a fine lady, tossing her curls as a pony tosses its mane, she was appealing and defiant by turns.

Maps were brought out, and the family began to discuss where we should go for skiing. Winterberg, we were agreed, was near, but its snow could not be relied upon, as it so often turned to rain. Johannes had heard there was a steady snowfall in the Harz, and that the surface was already firm. Therefore, on his recommendation, we shall almost certainly go there, to Sankt Andreasberg, the village already suggested by Selma and Kurt. We were sitting round the table, with the maps spread out, looking at the Christmas tree whose candles Johannes had just lit, when Herr von Ravenstadt gave a sigh. As he looked up at the illuminated boughs, he said something which I could not catch, but for the name 'Brita'. A shock ran round the room; I glanced first for Helga. I had forgotten she was still upstairs resting. I looked at Klaus, who had turned sharply in his chair, and was leaning forward, towards me but not seeing me. His eyes were fixed in a dead tormented gaze. Nobody said anything; Klaus seemed to have become oblivious of the rest of the room. Feeling someone's gaze, I glanced up to encounter Johannes's eyes, which were going from me to Klaus and back again to me. There was something shrewd and alert in his face which I had not suspected him of displaying. I had taken him to be a simple unobservant soul. Now I began to change my mind, as I suddenly realized he must be aware of the strong link between Klaus and myself. Sighing, he raised his body, and turned round to the blond young man, who sat away from the rest of us, saying:

"Why do you not speak to our guests? You can speak English."

To Antoine he said: "He was a prisoner of war in England. He understands the language."

The man muttered under his breath, but would say nothing to us.

Herr von Ravenstadt began to busy himself with preparations for a punch which he was going to make for dinner. He put an iron pot on the stove, from which the heat was almost suffocating. Sidi was becoming restless.

41

"The heat is unendurable," she declared. "I must go for a walk before dinner or I shall not sleep tonight."

She asked me and the woman friend who had come in with her father-in-law, to go for a stroll as far as the autobahn.

There was a sharp frost on the ground, and a pallid new moon above the black and absolutely silent avenue. Sidi thrust her hands deep into her pockets as she strode along.

"I love to walk. I like exercise. It kills me to be indoors over the hot stove the whole day."

For the most part I was quiet, enjoying the cold air, watching the stars and the moon. We paused on the bridge over the autobahn, to watch the traffic passing beneath.

"They have made a new regulation: Johannes has just heard about it. Tractors are not to be allowed to go on the autobahn."

As we walked down the house-field, Sidi told me how it was that they had been able to rent this property.

"The people who lived here were old; they had two sons who ran the farm. One night, when they were sitting quietly by the stove in the living-room, their Polish servants came outside the unshuttered window and shot them dead. For a long time, the land was vacant until we took it."

After the night air, the living-room was more unendurably hot than it had been before, and the yard inside the house-doors was as cold as the air outside. Now, sitting in the panelled room, in the security of family life, with the decorated tree's fragrant branches speaking of the Westphalian forests, it seemed impossible that hatred-maddened men had taken aim through those wide innocent windows, that dead bodies had lain in pools of blood on this floor. Who was our enemy, to creep on us unawares?

The blond young man whose name I did not know, was sitting head in hands before the fire.

Helga, rested but still looking troubled, came into the room. The young man dropped his hands, raised his head, glanced round as if trapped, and rushed from the room.

Inser had avoided me since my arrival because her parents had begun to tease her to sit next to me and make English conversation. She came to me now, seeming to have made up her mind; approached with confidence, and began to show me her paintings, paintings of the farm, herds of horses, and skiers rushing downhill between forest trees.

It was long past the children's bedtime when we sat down to dinner in the long dining-room. I sat between Herr Ravenstadt and Inser; Antoine sat next to Helga at the other end of the enormous table. We were twelve: at tea we had been thirteen with the blond young man, who was now absent. Herr von Ravenstadt went round the table, ladling the hot punch into our glasses. He was gallant to me: "The drawing you made, the self-portrait when you were a student; the one you sent to Klaus, it was a good drawing."

"Where is it now? He has not still got it, has he?"

"No, it was left behind in Schlotheim. The Russians have it now. Perhaps Herr Stalin put it on his bedroom wall."

He laughed immoderately at his own joke. A happy-natured man, full-blooded and witty, he grew more garrulous with the punch. He kept raising his glass to Antoine, shouting:

"Monsieur Antoine, I drink your health."

Helga, with a painful smile on her face, made a few

remarks that were received in silence. Her smile grew more and more strained as the meal progressed. Kornelius, beside himself with joy at being with the grown-ups so late in the evening, sipped at his father's glass of punch: his cheeks became more than ever flushed, his eyes burned star-like.

We all helped with the washing-up afterwards, because the maidservant was away for the holiday. The kitchen with its tiled floors and iron cooking stoves was like an ice-box.

Kornelius rushed, screaming with terror and over-excitement, into the kitchen, and flung himself onto his mother. His father had just told him to go to bed.

"This happens every night," said Sidi. She held him close, trying to quieten his wildly-threshing limbs.

"The thought of being put to bed sends him into hysterics."

"Kornelius, Kornelius," cried Herr You Ravenstadt, rushing after the child; "I will take you up to your room: there is nothing to be afraid of."

Still screaming and struggling, the little boy was carried into the front hall towards the stairs by his mother, followed by the grandfather.

It was about eleven o'clock when Klaus went out to hitch Albrecht to the cart, accompanied by Inser, pale with fatigue. At the last moment, the dog Jula could not be found; Inser and Justus had been dressing her up during the afternoon in scarves and jackets until she was so bored that she ran away. Klaus found her, curled up asleep in a corner of the stable.

The basket chairs were put in the cart; Helga clutched the struggling Jula to her breast; Albrecht plunged and twisted, trying to bolt, to smash the cart into the fence. At the last moment, Inser cried out: "Uncle Klaus, Uncle Klaus, you have no lamp."

He laughed, but asked for a light. Johannes brought out a tiny lantern in which burned a weak flame. This was handed to me as, for the first time, I was to ride beside Klaus, so that Helga should have the comparative comfort of a chair. Finally, we were away, the horse plunging forward wildly on the steep field path leading to the road.

On the main highway Klaus pointed out a place where the horse had bolted downhill with the wagon full of children.

"I threw the children out one by one into the road, all except Kornelius who was very young. He curled himself at my feet and did not cry or say a word."

Albrecht was lively and capricious in Herford, and I could sense Helga's fear. The black bulk of the caserne stood on our left, to which a few British soldiers were hurrying. Antoine, to Helga's delight, began to sing French songs.

Later, Antoine said to me: "Did it not seem strange to you that nobody came out to say goodbye when we left Schwarzenmoor?"

I was awakened violently during the night by the sound of feet running upstairs, and Anni's voice calling her mistress. She knocked at the door of the next room. After talking together, she and Helga went downstairs, and I fell asleep again.

At dawn I was again disturbed, by the sounds of loud voices in the next room. The quarrel seemed to be on Helga's side: her voice rose and fell, becoming tearful and desperate. After Klaus had gone downstairs, and I was washing, Helga

45

tapped on my door. There were no traces of tears on her face. She said abruptly:

"You must pay no attention when we have words. It is marriage."

NEW YEAR'S EVE

WE did not stay up until midnight to welcome the New Year, though we celebrated in the evening by eating a dishful of doughnuts made in the afternoon by Helga. While she used the rolling pin I put on each circle of dough a spoonful of jam. The heat from the wood-burning stove was so fierce that I had to wrap a cloth round my arm to prevent it from blistering.

At about ten thirty Antoine left us to go to his bed at the other farm. Anni has the night off and will be away tomorrow, so Klaus slept downstairs in the nursery in case the babies cried during the night. While I was speaking to Antoine at the front door, Klaus went past us with a book and a blanket. We were laughing at something Antoine had been saying. Klaus said good night, opened the living-room door, and I turned to see his back silhouetted against the light of the room beyond. He looked more than usually tall, upright, and lonely. Something about his appearance made me stop laughing.

Oma and Opa are packing their belongings in readiness for leaving for another farm. Oma is old and has a bad heart; she cannot face another summer of hard work in the fields. They have had the good fortune to find two rooms,

46

far better ones than these, in another farm a short distance away. They will have left the Schäferhof by the time we return from the mountains. It will probably be a relief for them to get out of this 'madman's house'.

Today it was brought home to me that Klaus has a streak of madness. At breakfast, he suggested that we should go for a morning drive in the wagon, to visit a small church on a nearby hill. At first, Helga said she would stay at home, as she is growing more heavy and fatigued each day; then she decided to come, at the last minute. Gottfried has been sickly and fretful since our arrival, so he was left at home, but Klaus insisted that Angelika should go with us in her wicker-work perambulator. He lifted the pram containing the child into the wagon; afterwards leaving the horse to stand unattended at the door. Albrecht began to walk out at the open gateway. The rumble of wheels set the house in a turmoil: the women screamed; Anni, Helga, Oma shrieked, "My God! My God!". Opa appeared at the door, a fat cigar clutched in his hand. There was uproar until Klaus went out and stopped the horse. Helga could be heard complaining fretfully from indoors. Klaus beat the horse with the knotted rein until he had mastered it. Angelika made no sound; only peeped round the hood of the pram at me. Klaus was standing at the other side of the cart close to the horse's head. I could hear him cursing under his breath. He muttered in English:

"What an awful girl, what an awful girl."

Helga, the object of his curses, came out into the yard, and still complaining, climbed into the cart. Antoine and I had to squeeze beside Klaus as the pram and the chair took up all the space behind.

The earth was in the grip of an iron frost. The sun shone brightly in a limpid blue sky in which floated small round clouds like loaves of bread. There were traces of snow in the fields, and ice in the wagon ruts. It was pleasant weather; the little dog had come along and was enjoying herself scenting for hares. Antoine and I walked for part of the way, preferring to exercise our limbs rather than to be crowded together on the seat. Klaus and Helga looked happily harmonious with their daughter in her carriage.

On the way home, Klaus's mood changed unaccountably. He took to the field tracks, in which the ruts were hard as iron. Helga could not bear the jolting, so she got down into the road. Without anyone to steady the pram, it slid about the cart floor, threatening to overturn. Helga stumbled after the wagon, panting and shrieking for Klaus to stop and let her get up again beside the baby.

"No, no. It is bad for you. Let me get in." I seized her arm.

Klaus looked back over his shoulder. Seeing my determination, he reined in long enough for me to get in beside the child; then he set off once more on his insane progress through the countryside. Antoine and Helga were left far behind. I went down on my knees and put one arm across the pram to prevent the child from being flung out onto the ground. Angelika was silent, though she was being tossed about so violently that I thought she would become insensible. She seemed to be half-stunned by the shocks. I was horror-stricken by Klaus's brutality, and terrified for the safety of the child. I looked at the man's back, and realized that silence alone could save us from accident. Once, the cart went far down on the side where the pram was, in a deep furrow, and I thought we would overturn, but the cart was dragged out again onto level ground by the half-frenzied horse. Klaus turned round once or twice, grinning at me as if over a shared joke. Once, I tried to protest, not about his treatment of Angelika, but about Helga.

"It is dangerous for her. She might be seriously injured."

"Yes, yes. She should stay at home."

A pain burned in my chest from bending over the pram. My knees were sore, my arms and head ached. At last we turned into the yard, almost taking off the gatepost; the horse stopped, quivering and sweating, before the house. In silence, quite out of breath, I helped Anni to take the bemused Angelika into the house. The baby's hands were very cold. It was five minutes or more before the others reached the house. Helga, her face ashen, her breath coming with difficulty, went to the living-room. As soon as she had the baby in her arms, she began to weep.

"It frightens me. It is terrible. I am always afraid in the cart."

The pain in my chest was nearly suffocating me. Between the double glass of the window stood a bottle of beer, put there to keep cool. Opening the inner window, I took out the bottle, and drank from it.

At lunch, Klaus scarcely spoke. His face wore a look with which I am beginning to be familiar, the look of a soul in black torment. Instead of taking his customary siesta, he rushed out in the direction of the little wood.

Helga, serene once more (her sombre moods are quickly past and forgotten), laughed.

"He will be back for afternoon coffee. Perhaps he has gone to the Obernburg to wish them a happy new year."

It was dusk when he returned, still in the same morose temper, which persisted throughout dinner. At the end of the meal, Helga went into the next room and came back with Angelika in her long white nightclothes. The child was stupid with sleep; but her mother bounced her on her knee, until she was fully awake. She was showing off the child to gain the attention of her husband. He would not yet be won over; his glazed stare passed her by.

As usual, we spent the evening upstairs. Helga brought Angelika too; remorseless now in her determination to win smiles from her husband. At last, he could stand it no longer; the child's ways were too winning to be disregarded. She ran up to his knee and stood there, gazing at him, her body tense with the effort to remain upright. His face slowly relaxed as, with a laugh, he lifted the child onto the divan and began to play with her.

Helga has told me that when she protested to Klaus about his wild driving, he only said: "There was no danger. Elizabeth was in the cart, looking after Angelika."

JANUARY 1

AT the end of the wood is the larger Schäferhof, where another of Klaus's cousins lives with his fat wife. This house too is overcrowded with friends and relations from the east. Klaus calls this cousin "the wickedest man in Germany". At the end of the war he had a comfortable position as chauffeur to a British officer. The house is close to the road, alongside Klaus's large field of brussels sprouts. When we are out there picking sprouts for market, as we do nearly every morning, I always feel that we are being watched from the house. Klaus has no desire that we should visit there, and he sees little of them; but today he went to wish them a lucky year.

The brussels sprouts have to be carefully prepared for market. It used to be possible to send them as they were picked from the stalks; but now they have to be trimmed carefully with a knife, and the outside leaves removed. They are cold things to handle. We tip the green mounds onto the kitchen table and then spend the morning trimming, until we wish never to see a sprout again. To Antoine's disgust, they form a staple part of our diet. When they have been prepared, they are taken to the Obernburg where they are weighed, put with the other produce, and sent to market.

Kurt came to collect a sack of them in his car, which is a small two-seater. The sack was stowed under the seats. Helga sat beside Kurt; Antoine and I packed into the dickey, and we bumped off down the road. Klaus ran round beside the wood to meet us on the main road. He was carrying the gun he had borrowed for the hare shoot.

I thought my face would be frost-bitten, it was so cold in the back of the car. Having splashed through the muddy lane in safety, Kurt stopped to pick up Klaus. He pulled a rug over my face to protect it from the wind.

After the vegetables had been weighed in one of the farm buildings, we went into the castle. We all entered at the door leading to Selma's apartment, with the exception of

Helga who went in at the right hand door, saying she was going to see her sister.

In the evening we played a noisy game called Quick Quick Six Six. For this game, Selma produced a pair of skiing gloves, an old hat, a scarf, a knife and fork, and a block of chocolate wrapped in brown paper and tied with string. The game was simply to throw the dice: anyone throwing a six had to put on the gloves, hat and scarf, take the knife and fork and untie the string with these, unwrap the paper, cut the chocolate, and get a piece up to the mouth, using the knife and fork. While this was going on, the dice was being thrown by the others round the table. The first to throw another six had to snatch the objects, and so on, until the block of chocolate had been eaten. It was a noisy game, and very warming. Seven of us played: Selma; her mother, the two children, the three of us from the Schäferhof. Kurt stood behind to watch. I almost asked why he did not play; for the moment I had forgotten about his empty sleeve.

We relaxed afterwards, completely exhausted, and drank wine together.

"Where is Helga?" I asked Klaus.

"I do not know," he replied without enthusiasm; "I have not seen her."

"She must have gone home in the car with Sophie or the chauffeur," said Kurt.

Selma opened the double windows. Beyond the moat, a thick hoar frost was showering onto the trees. The moon was infinitely high in a black heaven, and reflected wanly in the frozen lake.

Once again we had come out without a carriage lamp, but

it was midnight and the moon was high; so Klaus said we could risk going home without a light.

"We'll go by the path along the Verre!"

The Hastfers laughed. Kurt said, looking at KIaus with affection:

"Old Klaus is an original."

Despite the moonlight, the night was not clear. The three of us packed ourselves together on the driving seat. Klaus put his left arm round me; from time to time he stared earnestly into my eyes, but he said nothing. The landscape was vague, impalpable; the trees were a flat grey screen against the silent Verre.

A light shone in Helga's room to welcome us as we came out of the clutching boughs of the Schäferhof wood. The light went out as we were crossing the field to the house.

A plate of fruit had been placed on the table by my bedside. So ended the first day of nineteen hundred and fifty three.

JANUARY 2

THE arrangements for our skiing trip have been completed. Tomorrow morning we leave, for a three weeks holiday in the Harz Mountains. Almost the whole of that region is now in Russian hands; only a small area is in the British zone, so we shall be within a few miles of the Russians.

Antoine is to borrow Klaus's skis; Helga's are too long for me, so I shall have to hire mine in Sankt Andreasberg. The train leaves Herford at nine o'clock tomorrow morning (there is a special portion for skiers on Saturdays), arriving in Goslar at about one o'clock in the afternoon. A bus will take us up into the mountains; we should reach Andreasberg at about dusk. It does not yet seem possible that we shall soon be in mountains and forest.

Selma asked me to spend the last day before our departure with her at the Obernburg.

Today I must find out about Brita, I told Antoine, because I hoped Selma would tell me everything I wanted to know.

There was a battle of wills before we left the Schäferhof. We were to leave early so as to be at Selma's by breakfast-time and Klaus was determined to take me in the wagon. The frost has grown every day more severe, the cold more intense, the landscape wintrier. Antoine was to accompany us; then the two men were going on to Herford.

Helga was helping Anni to wash clothes. She kept drying her hands, in order to run after Antoine or Klaus, whichever was near, to try and persuade them to go by bus and not with the horse.

"It is madness to go out when the roads are so hard for the horse's hoofs; they will crack. And you will die of the cold."

She begged Antoine to speak to Klaus: "He has never been so crazy, wanting to go out every day with the horse in this bad weather, and Herford is such a long drive."

Disregarding her, Klaus brought out the horse, and harnessed him.

"You can go by bus to Herford; I shall take Elizabeth to the Obernburg and join you at the reise-bureau," he told Antoine. My husband said he preferred to go by cart, though I know he hates to sit behind the unpredictable Albrecht.

Selma was not at home, having gone to the hairdresser's at Herford. She would not be back until lunch-time, but Vivica was waiting to take me for a walk in the forest. So I found myself for the second time walking through the deserted garden and up towards the forest. The child and I spoke in English, because she is eager for new words; snatching at them, trying them on her tongue, storing them up in her quick mind.

The forest was silent and deserted save for one man who passed us, bicycling down a steep glade towards the castle. When she saw him, Vivica drew closer to me.

"He is a clown," she said, "who steals wood from the estate."

Despite myself, I could not prevent a shiver running down my back at the sight of the forest, dark and secretive. I drew nearer to Vivica, looking around me, half-expecting to see a figure lurking in the undergrowth.

"Mammi forbids us to go alone into the forest," said the child. "But when our friends come, we are allowed to play there. Our dogs come with us."

There was an open space at the top of the hill, on which stood a look-out tower. I recognized the landscape below us: it was where we had joined the huntsmen on the hare shoot. Peasants were at work on the stony earth.

When we came in from our little tour, we found Kurt eating from a tray in the living-room. He kissed my hand, saying:

"Ah, Miss Elizabeth, you have roses in your face."

He shared his sandwiches with me, and called to his mother-in-law that she should bring me coffee. Peter Christian and Vivica brought a dish of nuts.

"Selma telephoned," said Kurt. "She met Klaus and Antoine in Herford, and is coming back with them in the cart."

After lunch, the grandmother made me take a rest. She covered me with a warm rug on the divan in the room with the Christmas tree. She kissed me and left me alone. I was already drowsy when voices and footsteps on the stairs roused me. The three burst into the room, laughing and shouting. The sharp smell of clean frosty air came from their clothes. Klaus was flourishing a bottle of schnapps.

"Hush," warned Selma's mother. "Can't you see she is resting? She has been for a long walk in the forest with Vivica."

"Oh," exclaimed Klaus, pursing his lips in mock pity; "Poor little Elizabeth, you must have a drink of schnapps. It will make you sleep, and warm you. It is a good drink."

"No, no. I am sleepy enough already."

He measured out the drink into a small glass, brought it to me, and stood by me while I drank it.

Selma's vitality was an electric force in the room. Her husband made her spin round so that he could admire her new hairstyle. She bent over me, laughing: "But come; you will not be able to sleep here with the noise. You shall sleep on my bed in the other room, with the door shut. First, we will eat. Then these noisy fellows will go away, and I can have my siesta. Afterwards, you and I can be alone together."

She took me to lie down in the far room; covered me up, and kissed me as her mother had done. She burst out laughing when she saw how little space I took up on the divan.

"Why, you are no bigger than Vivica: you are only a child!" Their voices, the sound of knives and forks, made a muffled, comfortable background to thought. A photograph of a dead wife, tall windows steamed by heat, dark carpets on the floor and on the walls, first editions stacked on the desk, sketch books, engraved goblets, a few pieces of china, are all that are left of a way of life, of a culture. The mouldy ceiling is mapped with damp patches.

I feel that I am home; it is wonderful to be at home and loved; not only by Klaus, but by the whole circle of friends, Sidi, Johannes, Kurt, Selma and the others; whereas on the island I feel more strongly each day my exiled state.

Each of us inhabits his own world and all our worlds are unreal. These people, deprived of their lands and homes, are sustained by memories of the past; they live for the immediate present too, the fancy dress party, the dance, the birthday celebration. Of the future, they speak but seldom; when they do, it is with dread of the Russians, and of what they may do next. They have no future such as they were born to expect. Klaus, for example, was a doctor of law; he took a degree in forestry too, in order to be fitted for the life of a landowner. He was the lord of Schlotheim. He talks at times of past pleasures: carp pools, rose gardens, horses, foreign holidays, tutors, nurses.

His friend Kurt Hastfer earns at the present time the equivalent of five pounds a week as steward of the Obernburg.

Helga, perhaps because she is shallow; perhaps because she is wiser than the others, talks frequently of, "When Klaus returns to Schlotheim we shall be rich." I cannot believe she will ever be the mistress of Schlotheim. Forcing myself to be honest, I know it disturbs me to think of her as its mistress. Of Brita, whom I never met but of whom I heard so much in letters, I was never resentful. It has become quite clear in my mind; since Brita cannot return there, then it is for me to go. Schlotheim is part of my myth-inheritance. It would be as familiar to me as the Obernburg is familiar; I could walk out onto the terrace from the cool interior and know the individual shape and colour of each flower hanging between lacquered leaves. The ripe wheatfields would smell like the new bread peasant women carry home on two-wheeled carts from the baking oven in the village. I thought of Thuringen, the green heart of Germany, that with its hills, its charcoal burners' huts, its farms, has become part of me.

I must have slept for nearly two hours. Once, just as I was dozing off, Selma came in and told me that the men had gone. She was about to take a rest in her mother's room.

The sound of the door opening roused me. Vivica looked in, hopeful that I was awake. I must have looked discouraging, because her head was withdrawn at once. She left the door ajar, and I could hear her giggling and whispering with Peter Christian in the next room. Reluctantly, I got up. The girl had kept an eye on me all this time; when I stood upright, she leapt into the room, pigtails swinging, and caught my hands.

"Come with me; I will show you our chapel, decorated for Christmas."

"Where is your mother?"

"She is resting in grandmother's room. Please, come with me to the chapel."

On the ground floor was a long tiled corridor, with high windows looking into the courtyard on one side, and on the other side, doors. Vivica opened one of them, and at first I could see nothing. When my eyes grew accustomed to the gloom, I saw a bare altar on a dais, vases of flowers before it, and chairs placed in rows for a congregation.

"We came here on Christmas night," said the child. "Fräulein von Dorn's brother used to read the lessons, but now he is a prisoner in Siberia. Look, it is damp, but there is no money for repairs. How musty it smells. The Obernburg is unhealthy and damp because it stands in the water."

We went out and closed the door. Along the wall at intervals, stags' antlers thick with dust, hung on wooden shields. I glanced at the door next to the chapel.

"That is where Klaus and Brita used to live," said Vivica. My heart began to beat painfully, because I had no wish to see the room. I rushed past the door and towards the stairs, with the child following me.

Selma was putting coffee cups on a small table.

"We will have coffee alone," she said; "without the children. Then we can speak together in peace. So you are going tomorrow to the Harz? And will Klaus join you there?"

"For the third week, I think."

"It will be good for Klaus. You must speak with him in the mountains."

"There is so much I want to know. I do not understand about Brita. He has told me nothing, and I am too shy to ask."

She stared at me in surprise. "You do not know?"

"No. Is she dead or are they divorced?"

"Brita died four years ago; her baby died too."

I got up, and went over to the silver-framed snapshot of the dark-haired girl, on the desk.

"Is this her picture?" I asked.

"Yes, it is a good one. She was full of fun and laughter. I like this picture more than the one Klaus has in his room; she looks so sad there."

I carried the photograph over to the table. While Selma told me the story, I studied the happy face on the piece of cardboard.

"She was a diabetic, and very ill before the baby came; but she wanted so much to have one. They had been married ten years and had no children. It was a great joy to her, preparing things for the baby. She and Klaus were happy: it was a good marriage. They only lacked a child. Because she was diabetic, she had to take injections. The child was born alive; it was a boy. The doctor had given orders that Brita should not be given an injection after the birth. She was left alone for a few minutes; she gave herself an injection. She died; and the baby died two days later. It was terrible for Klaus, they had been so happy. He felt that if only the baby had lived, it would have been part of Brita, something to remember her by."

"But now," I asked. "How is it with him? He and Helga, they are happy, aren't they?"

She shrugged her shoulders, and did not reply.

"They seem to be happy," I persisted. "And the twins are lovely."

At mention of the children, she responded eagerly.

"He has lovely children. It is not easy for Helga, because his first marriage was so happy, but it is lucky for her that

Brita's child did not live. It is easier for her not to have to look after the child of another woman."

"You will be quite near Thuringia when you are in the Harz," she said suddenly. "You must be careful to watch Klaus when he comes to Andreasberg. It is seven years since he left Schlotheim. He will be tempted to cross into the Russian zone and to try and find his way home."

"Do you think I could prevent him from going?"

"You must hold him by the hand to prevent him from doing anything foolish: he is quite mad. You must hold him by the hand. He might try to ski across the frontier."

I looked at my wrist-watch; it was time to start for the Schäferhof, since I was walking back, and I had promised not to be late for dinner. Selma said she would see me home as she wanted to give new year greetings to Oma and Opa.

It was a pitch-black night; fine grains of frozen snow were falling.

An aeroplane passed overhead as we were stumbling beside the railway tracks at the Obernburg station. Selma lifted her face towards the invisible machine.

"Two things I hate," she declared. "Aeroplanes, and tractors. My husband lost his arm in a civil flying accident before the war. Planes machined us on the roads when we were coming from the east; and a tractor was our home for six months on the trek." She added that the right hand of Helga's sister had been shattered by machine-gun fire on the way westward.

Our shoes broke thin crusts of ice. We were walking under trees: barely visible, they announced themselves by a desperate sighing.

Suddenly, Selma asked: "Do you find Klaus much changed?"

"No; scarcely at all. He is maturer, of course; but he is the same Klaus."

"Brita's legs became terribly swollen while she was carrying the child. They were discoloured and covered with sores. Klaus could scarcely bear it: he became more and more silent. After she died, he did not speak to anyone. He had to learn to speak again."

We walked on. It was not possible fully to open one's eyes. The hail cut and burned like knives.

"Did you write to one another during those years, Elizabeth?"

"Before the war, we wrote many times. Afterwards, I sent a letter to Schlotheim, without very much hope that it would reach him. It was forwarded from there to the Obernburg. He writes wonderful letters, the best I have ever received."

"In English, they are good also? In German they are beautiful. Did he tell you about the Russian campaign?"

"He wrote to me about it; about the horses, the snow and the mud; about an old peasant woman in the hut where he was billeted."

"Ah, he told you of the time in Russia."

The night seemed to grow darker and colder. Whenever a car passed us, we saw in its headlights bitter grains of sleet driven before the wind from the east, from the steppes.

"Helga is not satisfied with her life," said Selma.

"But Klaus and the babies... I am amazed."

"Yes, Klaus is a good man." At her words, I felt that the frost had broken on the fields, that the road was soft under summer dust, that there were flowers by the roadside.

"He is a good man." My heart sang.

"But Helga is fortunate. She has three servants, and it is such a small house, the Schäferhof. She has very little work to do. She is not happy to bear children. I am different; I am happy when I am going to have a baby," said Selma.

It seemed unbelievable that Helga should not wish to bear children to such a man.

It was especially dark at the entrance to the wood; we groped our way along the path on its outskirt.

Antoine and Klaus came to the door, in response to our knocking.

"Come upstairs," commanded Klaus. "Helga is resting in our room."

She was in her accustomed place, curled beside a shaded wall lamp. A hectic spot burned in each of her cheeks. She forced herself to greet me normally; asking if I had had an enjoyable day. What had I done? What had I seen? She barely glanced at Selma. She was evidently in a passionate rage, but whether it was because the horse had been taken out against her wishes, or because she disliked Selma, I could not decide.

"Are you excited about going away tomorrow?" she asked me.

"Yes, but every day in Germany is exciting," I replied.

Oma called from the foot of the stairs that it was time for the evening meal.

"We must go. Dinner is ready," Helga said, brusquely, heaving herself up from the divan.

There were places laid for five people, ourselves and Anni. The girl looked round the table, and in a faltering voice asked her mistress: "Shall I lay a place for Frau Hastfer?"

Selma had gone into the kitchen; I could hear her speaking with the Oma. "No," said Helga, "she will not be stopping for dinner."

The drawbridge went up on Klaus's face. With unseeing eyes, he stared at the colour reproduction of Dürer's *Virgin and Child* which, garlanded with flowers and evergreens, hangs outside the children's room. Selma was taking leave of the old people in the hall. As she opened the outer door to leave, Klaus got up violently from the table. He was only gone long enough to say good night to her. When he returned, he did not look at Helga who, for her part, kept her eyes on her plate, smiling to herself with the Gioconda look.

While I was packing in preparation for morning departure, I took my silk dress in for Klaus and Helga to see.

"That will do for dancing," Klaus said, in a muted voice. He had spoken several times in anticipation of our dancing together but now, before his wife, he showed no interest. He has told me several times, "We will dance on the first night I come." It is useless for me to protest that I know nothing of dancing.

Here, it is never peaceful. There are the ugly sounds of heavy transport on the Löhne-Herford road at the edge of the Schäferhof wood; and the wailing of the babies; Helga's querulous voice; and the stamping of the horse in its stable under the bedrooms.

Yesterday, Klaus said to me: "Will you take the cyclamen with you to Sankt Andreasberg?"

2

OBERHARZ

JANUARY 3

OUR arrival and reception in Sankt Andreasberg was unpropitious. It was a shock, after being in the shelter of Klaus's friendship, to be flung out into an uncaring world. Klaus went with us to Herford, and saw us onto the train.

At Hannover, the compartments filled up with skiers. So far, we had seen no sign of snow-hills. We were travelling through a flat uninteresting countryside; my excitement faded. Surely there could be no good skiing anywhere near. At one o'clock we reached Goslar, a mediaeval town made magically beautiful by a light sprinkling of snow. We had to wait two hours for the bus to take us into the mountains. The town was full of skiers, many of them leaving the station for the high villages; the rest coming to the station had the unmistakable snowlight on their faces.

We wandered in the old town, admiring the tall Gothic houses. At three o'clock we boarded the bus; skis and sticks were piled onto the roof. The first intimation that we were really going into high country came when the driver, a nervous-looking person, ordered a passenger to remove his heavy suitcase from the overhead rack. When the man protested, the driver snapped back, in a menacing voice: "Don't you know the Harz?"

Just outside the town, the bus stopped; chains were attached to the wheels; and we started the ascent.

We entered a narrow valley and began to climb, under an overcast sky towards a distance lost in snow-haze. We were in a black and white world; black tree trunks, black river, white earth, white-capped boulders. We crossed sensational bridges over mountain torrents. From the moment when we had left Goslar for this silent country of solitary escarpments and endless forest, we had been in the enchanted world of Goethe.

In such a new and thrilling encounter the life of the imagination is reborn. Deep in the gorge ran the black river islanded with smooth snow-capped boulders. Crags like those in Chinese paintings pierced the snow-fog. Trees under an immense burden of snow and ice groaned in the thin wind.

For nearly two hours we mounted steadily to the summit of the pass. A few sledges passed us, each one drawn by heavy Danish-type horses. The drivers were tough bearded men in fur caps.

From the summit we dropped abruptly between high snow-banks into the narrow village street of Sankt Andreasberg. It was already dark; the street lamps made pools of warm colour on the hard-packed snow of the road. It had been comparatively warm in the bus; the change of temperature struck at our bones as we stepped down onto the snow.

Along the street narrow lanes had been cut at intervals through the snow banks. Our bus had stopped in one of these gaps. In it stood a one-armed man in a thick leather coat. In his hand he held papers from which he shouted names. As they heard their names called, people stepped forward. The man spoke to them, giving the numbers of houses or names of hotels to which they were to go. Waiting beside him were small village boys with sledges. The children piled the luggage onto the sledges and set off to different destinations. We waited, thinking our names must be at the bottom of the list. The man read through to the end and turned away. We rushed forward.

"But where are we to go? We have booked at the Reise-bureau in Herford."

Our names were not down; nor were those of half a dozen others.

"There has been a mistake," said the man. "Will you please go to Hotel Bergmann for one hour—have something to eat and drink. In an hour I shall come there. Accommodation will be found."

Antoine took an instant dislike to the waiter in the hotel. We were both tired and cold and deflated, and extremely hungry. I ordered a black coffee; Antoine had a beer. The coffee gave me a certain measure of courage; the beer on an empty stomach made Antoine surly and arrogant. The waiter's large ears, and his servility, infuriated him.

There were eight of us in the hotel dining-room. If we looked as forlorn as the others, we must have looked lost indeed. The only cheerful ones were a blond wavy-haired young man, probably a factory hand, I thought, and his girl friend. She was a coarse-featured ruddy-cheeked woman, German from her Tyrolean hat to her boots. I remembered them from the train, which they had boarded at Hannover.

An hour and a quarter passed before the swing doors opened to admit the one-armed man from the bureau, followed by a small man carrying a large briefcase. The two officials consulted their papers, muttered together, and told us to follow them to the Reise-bureau. Outside the office was another group of small boys, with sledges. We were given directions, our luggage was packed onto a sledge and we followed our boy back up the village street. The address we had been given was that of Frau Schmidt, Schützenstrasse 99.

It was a yellow wooden house, one of a row, opposite the fire station. All the houses, we noticed, were built of wood. At number 99, the boy opened the outer door which set ringing a strident bell. Another door, glass-panelled, showed a polished staircase on the right, a long corridor on the left. The child shouted up the stairs. Then we called out. An old woman peeped at us from a doorway. We said we were looking for Frau Schmidt.

"Frau Schmidt? She is not at home. She expects no one tonight."

The deserted hallway was icy cold. Snow fallen from our boots stood in dry mounds on the polished surface of the floor. The boy, having received a tip, cried out "Good night" and ran off.

"What now?"

"God knows."

"I refuse to move another step." Antoine opened the front door and looked into the street. The front door of the next house slowly opened.

"Frau Schmidt?"

She was a short, pouter-pigeon-breasted woman, with big foolish eyes and an enormous beak of a nose.

"We have been sent by the Reise-bureau."

She had not been notified of our arrival, and she could not take us in. We grew roots into her polished floor, and refused to go.

At last, she was obliged to give in. It appeared that Frau Schmidt had already given up her own bedroom to a woman guest; there was a married couple in another bedroom; which left the small room where she had been sleeping. If we could squeeze in there for one night, she would make do on the living-room sofa.

"So: it is arranged."

The feather bed under us, the feather eiderdown over us, were unbearably warm, while the temperature of the room was well below freezing.

I fell asleep to the sound of sleigh bells.

SUNDAY, JANUARY 4

FRAU SCHMIT had moved our things into the double bedroom by the time we came back from skiing this evening.

Now at last I can begin to think over what Selma has told me of Klaus's private life. My relationship to him has taken a decisive step forward since my talk with her. In the bus on my way to the station yesterday, I was only able to say: "I wish you were coming too."

Before me stretches a fortnight of physical activity; while I struggle to master the nursery slopes, there will be time for contemplation. I am happy, mostly in anticipation of Klaus's visit. The thought of his coming spurs me on to keep up with Antoine who, because he learned to ski when he was a boy, is still good though he lacks practice. His graceful body vanishes down the misty slopes, and it takes me a long time to join him.

The village occupies a sloping depression in the hills. Nearby is a natural bowl which makes a good nursery slope. The bowl is tilted; the higher side of the rim adjoins the road to Sonnenberg and Goslar. Between this road and the rim, which is edged with small trees, stands the Hubertus Hütte. Opposite, the rim dips to a gentle field which gives access to the back lanes of the village. At the far end of the village is a railway line that comes up from the valley to its terminus, the station hotel where most of the skiers living like us, *en pension*, take their meals. A short distance from the Bahnhof, a steep road leads to the foot of the ski-lift on Matthias Schmidt Berg. To me, the Berg looks terrifyingly steep and complicated, particularly on the lower slopes. Along the crest of the Berg runs the bristling-black forest. At the top of the ski-lift is a Hütte with a tin roof weighted down with lumps of rock. In the middle of the roof is a tall iron chimney shaped like a woman: hat, tiny head, long thin neck, swelling bosom, pinched-in waist, and wide hips. She is braced to the roof by hawsers. Here, one can obtain coffee and cakes and steaming bowls of soup.

Today we discovered a small secret wood which must be one of those described to me by Vivica. Having been starved of the sight of trees and snow for six years, the time we have spent on the island, it gave us both the keenest pleasure to explore such a place. We saw a hare near a small stream in a private world of trees laden with snow that gave them fantastic shapes. From an invisible road came the sound of sleigh bells.

It has been a day of discoveries; some pleasant, others unpleasant. An instance of the unpleasant was afforded at lunch-time, when we went to the Bahnhof for the second time. Frau Schmidt had recommended the food.

Unlike last night, we found every table occupied. There was only one waiter, a middle-aged man with receding hair. The proprietor, large, paunchy, square-shouldered, handsome and red-nosed, stood behind a counter at the kitchen end of the room, keeping a strict eye on the tables, issuing commands to the waiter, and to his wife and the cook in the back premises. The room opens directly off the station platform, is centrally-heated, and becomes oppressively warm when there is a crowd in for a meal. There is a smell of food, damp clothes, and melted snow. Each skier as he comes in stamps on the mat, shakes snow from his shoulders, and hangs cap, gloves and ski sticks on the hat stand by the door. Skis are left outside on the platform.

Today the crush was terrible. Hundreds of people had come up for the day or for the weekend, to ski or simply to watch the sport.

We stood on the mat at the door, feeling unwelcome and abandoned. We had been out during the morning on the slopes; the mountain air had made us ravenous. Suddenly, I noticed across the room, the couple we had sat near in the train and in Hotel Bergmann. They smiled at us, and signed that they could make room for us on the bench where they were sitting, in an alcove at a round table with a crowd of other people. We tried to catch the waiter's eye. For all the notice he took of us we might just as well not have been there.

The slow minutes dragged by; under the clock was a hideous reproduction of a painting of full-blown scarlet poppies. I began to hate everything about the Bahnhof, particularly the painting.

An hour passed; we were still disregarded by the waiter. I began to think I had the answer.

"Antoine, it is because we are English. He is going to let us starve. He will not serve us."

The blond young man with the curly hair and his girl friend in the Tyrolean hat, heard us and understood enough English to catch my meaning. They too became indignant, saying: "It's because they are English."

Had I not been so hungry, I would have realized, looking round our table, that other people were much more upset than I was, and that they were all Germans.

"Herr Ober, Herr Ober." One woman in particular seemed ready to tear him into pieces. She raved, pointing towards the clock; he gesticulated, protested, and ran frantically from table to table.

JANUARY 5

NOW of course, we realize how abnormal Sunday lunchtime is liable to be in the Bahnhof: during the rest of the week, the dining-room is comparatively deserted. And since this is the third day on which we have put in an appearance, Herr and Frau Prass, the owners, have begun to treat us as honoured guests. It so happened that we had started by sitting at a table in a corner: this has now become our table. It is strange, how quickly one puts down roots, how quickly a particular table or chair can become part of one's life. Over the table is a photograph of a boy skiing on a sunlit slope. His body is silhouetted against a limpid mountain sky. Behind him are the rolling hills of the Harz, topped with forest. Above the table in the opposite corner is a colour print of a painting: *Napoleon in Exile*.

The blond young man and his girl friend come from Hannover. He works in a machine tool factory; an amalgamated British-German firm. Hans and Anita are typical lower-class work people. At first we thought they were married as they both wear wedding rings, but now Hans has told me they are still only engaged and will have to wait a year or two before they can afford to marry.

"I'd like to emigrate to Canada," he said.

Anita who, we have discovered, puts a veto on almost everything he suggests, made a discouraging sound.

They are crude, good-natured people, very shrewd about money, and full of self-interest. Antoine and I, from being with them, have coined a new phrase, a private joke: "looking for Anita". She is cautious to the point of standstill. At first, we had been led to believe by the way in which they both spoke of skis, bindings, waxes, the technicalities of the sport, that they were both experts.

This morning we went out with them for the first time. Like me, they had hired skis in the village. Anita immediately began to find fault with hers, though she refused to do more than stand on them.

Hans, whom we met by accident in the village, was carrying Anita's skis.

"They are no good for her," he said. "I am taking them back, to get another pair."

They joined us on the nursery slope; at least, he joined us. Anita spent the overcast morning rooted on her new skis under a tree on the rim of the Bowl. Hans's courage was amazing: though he had no knowledge of how to turn or control his body, his skis or his sticks, his keenness and zest for life spurred him on. With lashing arms and legs, he shot over the side of the Bowl. He fell every time, but scrambled up and tried again. When a snow fog hid our world, as it does almost every day, it was then that he began "looking for Anita".

There is an open-air crib in the village, under an illuminated Christmas tree. Frost glitters on the fine snow-dust which covers the head and shoulders of Our Lady and the bent backs of Saint Joseph and the Wise Men.

TWELFTH NIGHT, JANUARY 6

IT may happen anywhere; on the nursery slopes, in the forest topping Matthias Schmidt Berg, or on the fields outside the village; sooner or later, there will only be the three of us.

"Anita, where is she?"

Hans then says, very seriously, in his halting English. "I think I go; look for Anita."

This is generally the last we see of either of them until dinner-time at the Bahnhof when, reunited, they are to be found sitting side by side, their faces red with health. Anita depresses me infinitely. She sees faults in everything, from the food which is always too cold for her, to the contours of the landscape. She has a gesture of negation, flapping her hands in one's face, a gesture that strikes chill to the heart. She has no joy, only a dogged desire to see and do, always in moderation, what others have seen and done. She is cautious to the last degree. Her table manners are not far removed from those of a pig. He is the reverse. His motto is do or die. His face is always cheerful, his marcelled yellow hair is faultlessly parted under his ski cap, his chin is freshly shaved.

We took them by an easy route up to the corner of the forest on the east side of Matthias Schmidt Berg. On the way, we saw an extraordinary man coming down from the summit. He was lean, with a small white face, and was wearing orange knickerbockers and jacket, and a black ski cap that made him look devilish. On his back was an enormous rucksack. He sped down the mountain as if on wings.

Hans hurled himself at the slopes with gay carelessness; the girl remained at the edge of the trees, prey to a thousand forebodings. With these two people I feel my foreignness. We have no understanding of one another. The things that make for understanding in my world – painting, poetry, music – are unknown to them. When Hans expresses a belief in international peace, he speaks with a glib parrot-like voice, without real conviction. It is not his own thought, but shreds of opinion picked up on the wind.

They have tried to wean us away from the Bahnhof, having discovered an eating-house kept by two spinster ladies, near the top of the Street of the Nightshirts. It is a big house, death-cold and hideously furnished, with an iron stove, elaborately grilled, but without a fire in its belly. There is an ornate plush sofa which is the delight of our love-birds, who sit there for hours forgetful of aches and bruises. The food is served by a melancholy woman. Nobody else eats there: it is depressing to have the grim room to ourselves after the bustle of the Bahnhof.

Before dinner, Antoine and I went into Hotel Bergmann for a drink. Hans and Anita refuse to go near the hotels; though they are staying in a first-class pension, much grander than Frau Schmidt's house. While we were sipping our drinks, I felt eyes on me. Looking up, I was surprised by three small black faces pressed against the glass of the door. They were children dressed for carnival as the three kings, and they carried small sacks in their soot-blackened hands. With a yell, the big-eared waiter threw himself at the door, and locked it against them. Later in the evening the village was full of child masqueraders, dressed in bizarre garments: floppy straw hats tied with ribbon, gilt crowns, and tasselled shawls. They went into the hotels, private houses, and pensions, singing a traditional song. Sometimes they were favourably received with cakes and fruits and sweetmeats.

JANUARY 7

TODAY we persuaded Hans and Anita to come back to eating in the Bahnhof. There are two reasons for their preferring to go to the Street of the Nightshirts. They lack social confidence which makes them shy of eating in public; and the spinsters' house by reason of its lack of customers, is a good place for love-making.

JANUARY 8

ANTOINE seems to be delighted with Hans's company. It bored me after the second day. Antoine thrives on such shallow contacts: on people he will never see again, or people he can impress, he expends vast amounts of energy and goodwill.

He describes the island, he tells about lobster fishing and about the farm. While he talks, I spend the time thinking about Klaus, anticipating the fearful joy of his coming. I must speak alone with him while he is in Sankt Andreasberg.

JANUARY 9

SCARCELY a gleam of sun has pierced the snow clouds since our arrival. We ask, does the sun never shine here? There has been a gently persistent snowfall every day this week. White clouds like a giant's breath, black clouds like a pestilence, descend. The slopes are lost in a flurry of ice-burning flakes. A skier rushes by, a village boy, from the way he runs on his skis, lightly, with a dancer's grace, leaning now far to the right, then over to the left, in skating fashion. He slips through a whirlwind of snowflakes over the rim of the Bowl, and is lost in the cries and laughter of invisible beings in the pit.

So, it is winter in the Harz, and I am learning to ski. In my home mountains I had some practice each winter for ten years; but what with boulders and river beds and poor snow conditions, it was never possible to make much progress.

Impatiently, I look forward to skiing with my friend. We first met in mountains; we share a love of mountains. If that was all we shared, the future would be simple.

He has already said: "When we are together, we are at home. O, we love the sun and the hills, the sea and the sky, day and night, perhaps in a different way from other people; we can see the same things and feel and hear the same things, and so when we are together we are at home."

He went on to warn me: "Don't forget Antoine. You know him as a good man... Perhaps I am very bad, a terrible man."

Through the village, four-horse teams plod, dragging away cartloads of snow from the streets, or they are to be met with on an otherwise deserted track in the hills, carrying the wooden walls of a hunting lodge to be constructed in the snowy waste. The carts run smoothly on wooden sleds.

A carrion crow rose with a loud cry and a board-clap of wings from the side of a tree where it had bored two square holes into the heart of the trunk. Fine yellow splinters lay round the roots. This tree is one of a group on the edge of a plateau over which Antoine and I love to ski. The landscape is always vague up here. The plateau stretches away for many metres, and where it slopes gently away towards a valley, there is a hint of mist-garlanded trees. A hunting lodge is at the other end of the plateau.

A face peered at us as we passed the windows on our way down to the steep open slope. From here we often make our way back to the village by the road past the sanatorium, a long grey building that makes me feel I am in one of those nightmares where you try to hurry, and the more effort you make the slower go your feet.

I carry the weight of my thoughts up and down the dead-white shadowless slopes. I wonder how much Antoine knows. He probably guesses that I was prepared to leave him as long ago as last autumn. There is nothing left between us: our natures are too opposed for us ever to be close to one another again. And yet the fact of my need of him remains. Whether he needs me I do not know. On the slopes, he swoops past me effortlessly, with the easy movements of a mountaineer. He becomes identified with a roebuck glimpsed as it leaps across a clearing. The man is like the roebuck for speed; the roebuck is like the man when it pauses to look back over its shoulder through the waves of mist.

Above us, when we enter the forest, trees creak and groan in sudden changes of temperature; south wind bringing a soft thaw sends showers of ice and snow from the branches. A few hours from now it will freeze again, making the trees ghost-white. The boughs will become stags' antlers furred with frost.

Two nurses from the sanatorium were walking down the road. They were dressed in black; uniform, shoes and stockings, and handbags. One of them was leading a black dog.

A short distance out of the village, in the chalky landscape, off the Sonnenberg road, stands a hoar-grey watch tower, Jordanshöhe. It has slit windows and a snowy battlement. From the middle of the roof rises a narrow spire. Klaus is like Jordanshöhe, strong and solitary and enduring.

81

JANUARY 10

I WOKE up to the thought: "Klaus will come today." We have been a week in Sankt Andreasberg. At night, I dream of skiing down endless white slopes. It feels as if we had been in this friendly and unfashionable place for months rather than for one week. A big house up at the top of the Schützenstrasse is occupied by American soldiers. Occasionally, a busload of British and Canadians from other parts of Germany comes for a day's skiing on Matthias Schmidt Berg; but we seem to be the only foreigners staying hereabouts.

Hans and Anita left this morning. We went to the bus stop outside the Kurhotel to see them off. Yesterday, they returned their skis to the shop, and spent the last hours buying souvenirs and food. Anita bought trinkets; rabbits on skis, imitation edelweiss, and brooches for her family. For the first time she seemed to be happy when, just before they left, she showed us her purchases. I think she was glad to be going home, but Hans was melancholy and sentimental. He gave Antoine a tin of ski wax. Poor Hans! He would have been happy to stay the whole winter in the mountains. The holiday has not been too happy for him, with Anita grumbling and dissatisfied. His face was wistful as he waved goodbye.

After lunch we skied on a perfect surface (there had been a good snowfall) across the fields to a part of the forest where a wide steep path ran down to a gorge. Below us, on the hazy slopes, a ski-school was having its afternoon run. It was already dark by the time we reached the outskirts of the village; we had not been out so late before.

I was still downstairs at the back of the house removing frozen snow from my skis, when Antoine shouted to me, excitedly. Though at first I could not make out what he was saying, I knew, because of his tone of voice, and because of my morning premonition, that Klaus had arrived.

As calmly as I could, I called back: "I told you he was coming today."

Frau Schmidt was full of importance; "A friend of yours, a big man, has been asking for you."

"Did he give his name? What was he like?"

"No, he gave no name. He was a big blond man with spectacles. I told him you always came in about dusk. He promised to return."

"Klaus! It must be Klaus. It could be no one else."

Half an hour later, while I was in the bedroom changing for dinner, I heard his eager step on the stairs. He entered the next room where Antoine was sitting with Frau Schmidt. I did not join them immediately, for I had been surprised by such a flood of pure joy; so vibrant a sensation had run through me at the sound of his voice, that I could not trust myself to meet him. In the fight to control emotions, my fingers clung to the marble top of the washstand.

I opened the door. Klaus rushed towards me, brandishing a bottle of schnapps. "Isn't it marvellous?" he exulted. "Isn't it marvellous, that we could meet in the mountains?"

Frau Schmidt was afraid of the fine gentleman, and yet delighted by his informality. He was in his best clothes, and his green-edged hat was at its most acute angle, with the back turned up as he liked it and as Helga disliked it. He had on his fur-lined jacket, grey trousers, and pointed thin-soled shoes.

"They are famous in Westphalia," he bragged. "Everyone calls them my yellow shoes. Before I bought them, I had only a pair of broken boots."

He asked Frau Schmidt for wine glasses, and the four of us drank to the world, the snow, and ourselves.

The beautiful daughter of Hugo Prass was at the family table in the Bahnhof. Her mother and father dote on her; Frau Prass brings her tid-bits from the kitchen, and watches over her as she eats. She is a healthy young woman of great charm which she uses with effect when she holds court at her table, usually with three or four men-guests drinking and card-playing. Antoine and I have decided that two of them are her suitors. One is a policeman, the other might be a commercial traveller.

Everything is changed because Klaus is with us. The village has become magical, the lights of the Bahnhof burn more brilliantly.

"We must go dancing," commanded Klaus, as soon as dinner was over.

"I am too tired, and too stiff after skiing," I protested. When we promised to dance another night, he gave in.

"Show us the house where you are staying," said Antoine. We walked through the village past the Kurhotel and the hospital. The house where he had a room was on the opposite side of the road from ours. He pointed out his bedroom window, just clear of a snowdrift. As we passed the house, which belongs to the village wood-carver, we saw a group of men and women with suitcases standing before it. With them was the man from the Reise-bureau.

"More guests for Frau Hartmann," said Klaus. "There is nobody at home, she and her husband have gone drinking tonight."

They looked surprised when the tall stranger leapt forward, opened the door and with a flourish, bade them enter, before he disappeared with us down the street.

Frau Schmidt opened her eyes wider when we told her Klaus's family name.

"But he is a lord, an aristocrat," she marvelled.

JANUARY 11

AT last we can see the sky, which delights Klaus, particularly when we tell him it is the first time we have had sunshine since we came to the Harz.

"The sun is glad to see us."

It cleared slowly until, by late afternoon, the whole sky was blue, lightly dappled at the zenith with static fair-weather clouds.

In the morning we had taken the ski-lift to the top of Matthias Schmidt Berg. From the back of the Hütte we skied a long way through the forest.

Ready to break into spring, the twigs of a beech tree were encased in brittle ice clear as glass, and the leaves were packed into slender pointed buds protected by the frost.

"Let Elizabeth be our guide," called out Klaus, but I could be no guide to these two experienced skiers. They vanished ahead, and I struggled to follow them between the boles of the fir trees, a cold snow-dust on the face exhilarating as salt water. We climbed the summit of the next mountain and had a view over many hill folds and forests towards Thuringia. We were standing within the small zone of safety. From the Brocken westward ran the frontier. Below us lay the area of no-man's land cleared of timber. With an intense gaze, Klaus looked towards his homeland.

Turning to me with a smile, he said: "Shall we go? We could cross the frontier at night."

Would it really have been possible to walk through the decayed, snow-levelled garden of Schlotheim, past the terraced walls with their statues and urns, into the house with its canopied four-poster beds? Would my self-portrait, given to Klaus twenty years ago, still be hanging on his study wall?

We returned to the Hütte for lunch; it was overheated, and snow lay in pools on the floor. Condensation streamed down the walls. A soup cauldron on top of the stove was ringed with wet gloves.

When it was time to descend into the valley, the men took the direct way down, while I went gingerly, making an easy traverse to the corner of the forest.

The village was full of sightseers gathered for the ski-jumping. The sky was still clearing with a wonderful calm slowness, which put us in such high spirits that we decided to have one more run before dark.

We were near Jordanshöhe when the sun came out fully a few minutes before it set. Alpenglow warmed the slopes, frosted boughs blossomed in an amethyst air.

Over coffee and cakes in the Hubertus Hütte, Klaus and I sat on a sofa side by side, Antoine opposite us.

A vertical ray of light ran up the sky from the sun that was already below the horizon. Klaus said: "Sometimes the sun used to look like that in Russia."

We sped home in darkness, through the Bowl and across the gentle nursery slope, to change for dinner and dancing.

There is dancing on Saturday and Sunday nights above the Konditorei and Café Westerhausen in the main street. I was one of the few women in a dress; the others wore ski clothes. It was while we were in the inner room, drinking Mosel, that I noticed the change that must have been coming over Antoine since we were first in Germany. He was smoking cigarette after cigarette and his hands were shaking violently. Klaus was excited and gay, and he began to tease Antoine, asking him why he had not brought the charming daughter from the Bahnhof as a partner, thus giving point to the fact that I was his, Klaus's partner. After Klaus and I had danced together several times, he suggested that Antoine should take me on the floor. Antoine, his face rigid, refused. Klaus, seeing at another table a woman who was staying at Frau Hartmann's, went over and asked her to dance.

Antoine said in a dead voice: "I suppose we had better go on the floor."

It was impossible: he could not relax. His body, so used to exercise and usually so fluid in its movements, was now that of an automaton. Having stumbled together twice round the room, it was time to stop.

"What is the matter?" I cried. "Why cannot we keep in step?"

Klaus found us sitting in silence.

"I know I cannot dance," I burst out. "But I find no difficulty in following Klaus. He uses simple steps. Antoine, you are too complicated for me."

Klaus looked at me: "We are simple people. Antoine must find a complicated person as a partner."

Klaus and I danced together for the rest of the evening. He asked: "How old is Antoine?"

"Thirty-two."

"Oh, he looks older."

Then he said: "He is a nice person. I like him."

I was tired and troubled by this physical contact with Klaus. I was also aware of danger. I did not cease to think of Antoine sitting alone in the other room, and smoking too many cigarettes. What had happened to change everything? I who had not danced since I was a girl now found myself on the floor for every dance. Antoine the gay partner of so many other women sat alone with the air of one to whom dancing is a sin.

It was cold and clear and nearly midnight with one star shining, when we walked across the road to number 99.

I am oppressed by a terrible fear. Suppose that now in the mountains I should fall short of Klaus's expectations? I am not a strong or a good skier. Suppose he becomes out of patience with me, with my slowness and incompetence? Helga is an expert on skis. This morning he said, looking up at the mountain: "Helga would take the direct route down."

If, after keeping a friendship alive for twenty years, we should fail to sustain it when we are together, it would be a calamity. During this week, our sensitiveness to one another will be strained to the utmost. Our natures have not changed, but our minds and bodies have matured. We expect a great deal of one another, perhaps too much. Are we inhuman in our tenacity?

At intervals it is possible to relax in the miracle of having found one another again. There are difficulties we must climb over or sidetrack.

It seemed so easy on the face of it, his coming to the mountains. He even arrived a week sooner than we expected him; but when we were alone together for a moment, he told me of how Helga had tried to prevent his coming because Opa and Oma are moving to the other farm.

He is happy: incredibly and incomparably happy. We do not speak of the time to follow this joy, but live from day to day like pagans. His face shines with uncomplicated contentment.

At night he almost runs to his lodging in order to devour the night with sleep. In the morning he comes with renewed vigour to join us in another day of freedom.

JANUARY 13

SITTING at the breakfast-table this morning, facing the window with its homely view of a small tree with distorted branches and the roof of an out-house mattress-layered with snow, I tasted the staleness following too much night-thought.

Behind the forest, scarves and skeins of mist were being blown among the trees by the east wind.

Frau Schmidt stood in the dark corner between the sewing-machine and the wall, darning one of Antoine's ski gloves. She was crying quietly. Antoine was indifferent; he thought it was only eye-strain over the darning. Could I somehow have hurt her feelings? I had not enough German to ask her what had happened, and she seemed intent on keeping her sorrow to herself. I thought I knew what had caused it. The postman had come while we were still dressing. It must be bad news from her daughter in the Russian zone. The daughter and grand-children for whom she is always making garments, whose photographs cover the living-room walls, are her life and conversation.

She was out of the room when Klaus arrived, so I begged him to find out the cause of the trouble. When we were in the street, he told me the story. It appears that she has been applying unsuccessfully for three years to the Russian authorities for permission to visit her daughter and family in the proscribed zone. This morning she received yet another refusal. Only in the event of severe illness or the death of a relative will she be allowed to cross the frontier.

"The Russians don't want us to see how little food they have over there."

Though the Thuringian hills are far, they have a powerful magnetism for Klaus.

We ascended the mountain by ski-lift, sped through the forest, and climbed to the open slopes we visited yesterday. Klaus gazed towards Thuringen Wald.

His eyes became so fixed that I looked round the plateau for something that might distract his attention.

Smoke on the wasteland! It was pouring from the roof of a hut about a quarter of a mile to the eastward.

"What a strange hut."

"It's like a wigwam."

"No; more like a charcoal burner's hovel. They are made like that in Thuringia."

"Let us go there."

It was built like a wigwam, on a foundation of stout poles, but instead of being covered with skins, it was bark-walled. A rough ladder ran up one side to an aperture at the top out of which the smoke was pouring. A wide doorway partially covered with sacking faced the hills. Klaus called out. A voice answered from the interior. We stood our skis upright in the snow, and went in.

I had expected to see an old peasant crouched at his charcoal-burning.

There was a wood fire in the centre; over it, on a hook and chain hung a pot containing a thick bubbling fluid. Through the smoke I could see the figure of a young man seated on a rough trestle bed covered with skins. Under a fur cap, his hair hung over his eyes. A sheepskin-lined jacket was round his shoulders. He was leaning on one elbow, writing with a stub of pencil on dirty sheets of paper. Above his head was a hammock.

The three of us sat down on a bench against the wall. Beyond the pushed-back curtain of sacking rose the forest. There was a sound of firing from the Russian side of the Brocken.

The young man said to Klaus: "I am a research student. For two months I have lived here, preparing for a journey to Lapland."

"Who built the hut for you?"

"A peasant. It is in true Lapp style."

Antoine and the student ceased to exist for me. Klaus and I were alone on the snow-field. No longer need I cry, "Where are you, where are you?" We were back at the beginning of time, in a shelter of tree trunks and bark torn from the forest. The heat of the fire had softened the frozen earth around the hearth.

In the late afternoon we took coffee in the Hütte on top of Matthias Schmidt. The Hütte's electricity is erratic: each time a chair lands at the terminus of the skilift, it causes the lights to flicker.

We came down the mountain in half-darkness; a difficult time to judge the slopes. In one place, I prepared for what seemed a gentle descent, only to find the ground was level and hard as iron. I fell heavily on my side.

This was the first day on which I received praise from the men. At the foot of the mountain, as we were removing our skis, they told me I was improving.

We dined at Hotel Bergmann, which is more expensive and less interesting than the Bahnhof. If we miss a meal at the Bahnhof we find ourselves looking forward quite eagerly to seeing Herr and Frau Prass and their daughter. I have invented for the amusement of the others, a romance between Fraülein Prass and Herr Schubert the waiter. In my story, the waiter adores the high-spirited girl. His position will not allow him to voice his love; he can only smile sadly, a napkin over his arm, near her table.

Sometimes old men come to play cards with her father. The girl sits at table with them. Herr Schubert stands by, dreaming of the impossible. The girl glances up and laughs at him. He smiles back. Frau Prass, her mouth tight, her eyes darting, pokes her head out of the kitchen.

"Herr Schubert, someone is waiting to be served at the far table."

I have just remembered something that happened yesterday afternoon. We were on the flat crest of the Rehberg, preparing to go down to Andreasberg for the ski-jumping. The sky had a perspective of clouds to the westward. Klaus suddenly stopped, and put his head between his legs. When he straightened up, he said:

"It looks much more wonderful upside down."

I stared at him, a memory revived.

"I taught you to look at the landscape upside down," I said, remembering.

"Yes. Do you remember the lake and the sunset?"

"No," I answered. "Not any particular lake." In my notebook, because of its significance for me, I have made sketches of the Lapp hut. I have shown the interior and the entrance with the fire and cooking pot, the bench, the bed, the figure of a man sitting beside a woman.

JANUARY 14

EACH day we come a little nearer to the Russians, closer to the gunfire.

The mist broke into dazzling drops of moisture as we started along the road to the foot of the Rehberg, whence we toiled up through the trees. For me, the going was difficult. I had waxed my skis before starting, and I found myself sliding backwards. Antoine and Klaus with skins under their skis, could walk straight uphill. Trying to walk without my skis, I sank up to my thighs in the freshly fallen snow.

"Give me your skis. Climb onto my back," ordered Antoine.

When we reached the firm-packed surface of the track to the summit, he put me down and rushed ahead, looking neither to right nor to left. Klaus and I followed him, side by side.

The sky was of a brilliant blue, and the fir-trees were weighed down at their slender tips by masses of new snow. Dazzling hoar-frost covered the rounded drifts which flashed with green, red, and blue fire. From the trees above us, shining flakes of crystal dust fell through the air. There was no sound save for a faint hiss when a dry handful of snow fell.

I love Klaus as I love life, as I love the sun.

A clearing led sharply upwards to the summit. We rested in a level, sunlit space. Klaus took off his sheep skin jerkin, worn and ragged from the Russian campaign, and folded it into a cushion for me before lying full-length on his skis. I was looking at the past in motion before the forest, when I felt his eyes on my face.

Antoine was sitting some distance away. He called out:

"Look at the mist moving up through the trees. We must get away from here."

A cloud was rising swiftly from the valley. We ran before it through the forest until we came to a tall lookout post built of logs. An icy ladder led to a snow-filled platform: from it, we gazed across a spectral world. At this height, the mist was thin, but the invisible sun had attached pale shadows to the trees, so that they seemed to be no longer

94

trees but every kind of fabulous beast. They were leaning against the slope, and seemed to be in movement, and to be dragging their heavy bodies forward, with double shadows stretching far behind. There was a tall woman with a small head and trailing garments, and a spaniel was staring with dog-constancy over the heads of demons, countesses, and peasants. Huge dinosauri dragged their bony armour over the earth. Dwarfs, children, men, and beasts were moving towards the crest of the Rehberg.

We sped over an open slope haggard with tree stumps, while above the mist, sunlit and far away, swam the summit of Achtermann's Höhe, and further off, the Brocken.

Later, we crossed to our windswept plateau leading to the hunting lodge and the lovely run below; then home, past the sanatorium where men and women were waiting for death.

A wonderful mail awaited us: most of our Christmas letters and parcels, much delayed, forwarded on from the island. Letters from London friends betrayed a common mood of depression. There is an outbreak of illness in southern England, just as there is in Bavaria and in France. A parcel from the Obernburg contained two tins of meat, a long letter from Vivica, and two bars of chocolate for playing Six Six Quick Quick on wet days. Selma had made a drawing on the wrapper. It showed the three of us seated at a table playing the game, with the caption: "When the weather is bad and you are cold then you have to play the game Six Six Quick Quick."

In the afternoon, I rested on the bed for two hours, while Klaus and Antoine went out again to the top of the Berg;

Klaus to paint, Antoine to ski. They returned at dusk, in good spirits. Klaus had made a watercolour of the Hütte and the hills towards Thuringia.

JANUARY 15

TODAY I have been sitting on Achtermann's Höhe, the peak that yesterday looked so impossibly remote, within a short distance of the Russian zone. Yesterday, a scare had swept the village, a rumour that a woman skier had disappeared over the frontier. The incident has been reported in today's local newspaper. The truth appears to be that a married couple and their child skied over the frontier by mistake. They have been put in prison for a few days, and the husband has to pay a fine.

Sankt Andreasberg is permanently mist-enshrouded, but the road to Sonnenberg from Jordanshöhe sparkles always in sunshine. It is an exhilaration to come out of the vaporous mystery of the village to the frost and glitter of a different air.

At Sonnenberg the sun was so bright that it hurt the eyes to look at the dazzling fields. There was a tree covered with snow-buds against a purple sky.

At Oderteich, in a house at the head of the lake, we drank soup before setting out to climb the peak. A steep forest glade led up to the white egg-dome that protrudes from the forest. We were walking close together, traversing the smooth top, when Klaus said: "I am going to make a drawing. Come and sit beside me, Elizabeth."

Antoine hesitated, gave an impatient snort of disgust, and went on to the summit where other skiers stood admiring the view. Why should I not sit beside Klaus while he was drawing? It was what I had done many times before on Welsh hills. Antoine sat above, keeping us in sight.

From the foot of the forest a straight path ran across a gleaming snowfield into another belt of trees. Down there, a few small figures moved swiftly along the track. Opposite was the Brocken; at its foot, the no-man's land cleared of timber. The observatory on the Brocken was clearly to be seen; also, the ski-jump platform on the next hill, which was in the British zone.

A long perspective of thin cloud streamed away over our heads to a point in the southern sky. Before us stretched the infinite forests of the Harz. From the valley came the loud bark of a dog. A succession of rifle shots startled us. Whether they came from the British or from the Russian zone, it was impossible to guess.

Puffs of white cloud appear in the distance, swell up into fabulous snow peaks, and slowly disappear behind the horizon.

"Strange, it does not seem like twenty years... It seems no time at all. Do you feel that?" I asked.

"Yes exactly that." We gazed at one another, smiling with pleased surprise.

I could feel Antoine watching us.

"Klaus, will you tell me about Brita before we go back?"

"Yes." He did not look up from his paper.

"You know, you have told me nothing of what happened."

"No."

"Selina told me a little."

"Did she?" He looked up swiftly, then went back to his drawing. "I think we should join Antoine, or he will be angry."

Antoine was tense when we joined him; and derisive about "the drawing lesson".

The downward path was tortuous, with no clear runs, sometimes under low branches, once beside a huge boulder. I fell again and again. In some places it was like a switchback. The way widened, but was glass-slippery. We came out onto the open track I had noticed from above; a swift passage from darkness into sunlight. Our skis devoured the miles as we raced always downhill; on wide tracks moving with winged speed, a cold uprush of air freshening the face; sometimes finding a way among close-growing trees. Once, we had the prospect of a shadowed gorge from the edge of a cliff.

As always happened, Antoine was setting the pace, rushing forward as if engaged in a race.

Klaus stopped, and looked round him.

"Let us go more slowly," he cried out, as if in agony. "Why do you go so fast? We shall never again be here."

In a silent forest of tall firs we came upon the spoor of a herd of deer. A hillside dropped to a stream where the snow was soft and treacherous. This stream had to be crossed before we could reach the river Oder. At dusk we followed the road through the valley. The men were in front; I followed a short way behind.

In Oderhaus, a hamlet of foresters' houses, one of the foresters came up to us. He took us to see the deer feeding from racks of hay put out under the trees. A stag with massive antlers stepped among the boulders, followed by young and nimble deer. The forester told us we could obtain coffee in one of the houses at the far end of the village. A cheerful, big-lipped woman welcomed us into her house. Our gloves had become encrusted with ice, so that our hands ached from the cold. The woman hung the gloves on the front of the stove to dry, and told us we should have coffee presently. Her husband turned on the radio for us. The couple had no children, so they lavished their affection on a highly intelligent spitze dog. With a pure white coat from rolling in snow, and moist black eyes, he danced, shook hands, and with delicacy removed sweets from the mouth of his mistress.

I lay awake, remembering the past; going back over the many wrong turnings I have taken since the 'good time' of twenty years ago. In those days I had been his 'little sister'. He said tonight that his week with me is going too fast.

The wood-carver in whose house Klaus is staying, has a brother who runs the local newspaper, *Zeitung für St. Andreasberg*. Klaus has been talking to him about me. He wants me to write a short article about the village, to put in next week's paper. I love Klaus so much that each night I make a plan for the next day; which is, to tell him of my love. Antoine, as if he knew of my project, never leaves us alone together. I had thought there would be times when I could speak alone with Klaus in the mountains. Antoine said: "Yes, of course you must speak together," and redoubled his vigilance.

One afternoon, Klaus and I were so embarrassed at finding ourselves alone for a few minutes that we could say nothing; only look at one another.

Klaus has told me: after he had been wounded in Russia, he was invalided back to Eastern Germany, and whilst he lay in hospital, Brita was able to visit him every day. When the wound had healed, he joined her at Schlotheim. When the Russians overran the east, he and Brita fled westwards in a farm cart, with a servant driving. Though his wound had healed, Klaus was still lame, and a short time before, Brita had broken her leg. Only the servant had papers, for himself and wife. To get past the Russian guards, Brita had to pass as his wife, and Klaus as their servant. One of the guards was a woman. When she saw Klaus and Brita in the back of the cart, both with disabled legs, she said: "Poor devils; go on."

JANUARY 16

OFTEN, we hear a child crying in the house. Frau Schmidt owns the whole building, but only occupies the first floor apartment. The flat above is rented by a family with young children. The babies cry, but it is the sound of real weeping that disturbs me. It must be young Elko Stork from downstairs, the grandson of the old woman who first spoke to us at number 99.

Frau Schmidt often repeats to us the story of Elko. His mother is the unmarried daughter of Frau Stork. The girl had an affair with a British army cook garrisoned in the village. The child is regarded by the three women with pride and shame; as both glory and cross. He is perpetually teased by the women who cruelly threaten to send him to his father in England, under our care. We attempt to reassure him, but the torment continues.

When the other children are playing with their sledges and skis, he watches wistfully from the window. On Sundays, looking well-dressed and cared-for, he walks on the street with his mother. One afternoon, when I gave him a bag of bon-bons, he rushed across the room, and nearly knocked me over with the intensity of his embrace. In the evenings, he watches for us to come off the ski-run into the Schützenstrasse. In the misty dusk, the street lamps give a romantic, faint illumination. The drifts, pushed back each day by snowplough, are packed high against the trees of the avenue. Lights shine from the windows, and the street is filled with children. Only Elko is indoors, his face pressed against the inner pane.

Every night it snows, so that the trees have become over-laden. Even under the breath of a light wind, the giant firs groan and creak from their roots to the tips of their branches. If a high wind were to rise now, it would become dangerous in the forest. Burdened as they are, the trees would snap and fall.

Today, the Rehberg was fog-enshrouded. I went ahead of the others; Klaus came rushing up behind me in a sort of frenzy.

He cried back to Antoine: "She is always ahead of us. An angel, she flies to the peak."

We decided to eat our sandwiches at the house by the frozen lake at Oderteich, where we took soup on Thursday. A black stream ran beside the road, and emptied itself into the river that fed the lake.

New powder snow made the homeward run difficult, and we were in fog all day.

Klaus has sent a telegram to Helga saying that he will return home on Sunday, instead of tomorrow. Thus, we shall have an extra day together in the mountains.

JANUARY 17

BEFORE climbing the Bruckberg we sat, our skis and sticks forming seats, on the dazzling snow-field at Sonnenberg. It was the sweetest day, because in a sense it was stolen. Below the tree line, the snow had a glittering crust.

"Don't count the minutes and the hours on the clock," Klaus had cautioned me in one of his early letters.

I revelled in the stolen hours of this day, not looking beyond it.

We were kept aware of the presence of the Russians on the next mountain, from which the sound of firing never ceased. Jet plane engines roared but no machines appeared in the sky.

Lying on our skis, close together, we relaxed in the peace of one another's presence.

Goethe knew these mountains; Heine also.

In the forest, at midday, the fir trees were shedding their heavy garments, showering ice and lumps of snow on us.

The tops of the trees showed a startling green against the blue of the sky.

On the Bruckberg, a familiar figure was dancing on his skis. It was the man in the bizarre clothes who had gone rushing past us on Matthias Schmidt. He had a yellow, bony, chinless face, mad eyes, and a long thin neck with a protruding Adam's apple. He was wearing a black cap, the earflaps of which stuck out from his head. Plum-red knickerbockers and jacket, and black boots, completed his costume. When he saw me watching him, he danced with insane fever until I looked away.

Again, we made seats out of our skis and sticks. I sat on Klaus's sheepskin while the sun burned intensely on the surrounding peaks. A cloud-ocean lapped almost to the crowning forests; slowly sank when it reached the warmer air, and rose again. The afternoon went by in a timeless peace. Skiers passed in the middle distance.

Klaus said, "I was twice in Harzburg with Brita in springtime. Once before the war, once afterwards."

"You walked in the hills?"

"Yes. We were in Goslar too."

On the way home, we took the wrong turning, and were well on the way to Torfhaus before we realized our mistake. To regain the Sonnenberg path, we had to return to the summit. We followed an easy road downhill into cloud; then, on the flat, we came out into pallid sunshine at Sonnenberg. The sun hung low, monstrously inflamed.

Later, the heights cooled to an unearthly blue. The now familiar agony had taken possession of Klaus. It was as if he could not make me enough aware of the scene on which we gazed.

"Elizabeth, come here. Look: out there is an island with a lighthouse at the southern end. It is your island; look at the sea dashing against it."

It was true. The cloud was the sea, making an island out of the shoulder of the Bruckberg.

It was as if he wanted to press his face too closely against the landscape. What frightened me was that he wanted my face to merge with his. "Listen to the mermaids in the forest."

Under the trees, a brittle crust of ice had formed, which broke beneath the weight of our skis and was carried along by them. In some places the skis would not grip the surface, so that we slid and floundered.

It was now dark: the mist, which had an acrid smell, intensified the gloom, and hurt the throat. Klaus waited for me to join him. He put an arm round my shoulders, and drew me close.

"Un brave soldat."

We had another small hill to climb and then the long descent ending at the back of the Hubertus Hütte and the Bowl. Klaus led us down: I was put in the middle, and Antoine came last to see that I was safe. The night was now so overcast that I could not see the men, though I could hear the swish of Antoine's skis not far behind. I could not see my own hands, skis, or sticks. It was necessary to snowplough the whole way.

Klaus went to the Hartmanns' to change, before calling for us to go to dinner.

Every night, as soon as we are in the street, he takes my arm. On the first occasion when he did so, he asked Antoine to take my other arm, but Antoine refused.

104

"Oh, so you like to walk alone?"

"Yes, I do."

During the meal, we spoke of poetry and the difficulties of translating it.

"I should like you to translate my poems," I told Klaus.

"I should like to do it, but it is difficult work." He looked delighted that I had asked him.

"You, after all, are the one to do it. They are really your poems... Do you know, that hard-faced woman, Elko's mother, asked me the other day why I had no children."

"You should have told her that your poems were your children."

Tonight, he mentioned the article I must write for the *Zeitung*, saying he must have it by tomorrow morning to give to Herr Hartmann. He will translate it under the guise of a special correspondent.

He came back with us to the house to drink a bottle of wine we bought yesterday. He asked me for details of my life in such and such a year. Antoine made an attempt to interest him in his own past but Klaus, probably because he was tired after being out all day or because we are to part tomorrow, did not trouble to hide his boredom.

We return to the Schäferhof next Saturday. Our train is due to arrive at seven thirty in the evening, and Klaus has promised to meet us with the cart.

When we said good night, we shook hands formally with Klaus. As I turned away, he moved swiftly, again took my hand, held it behind him for a moment in a convulsive grasp.

KLAUS left at noon. It has been a terrible day. Immediately after breakfast, he came round to Frau Schmidt's. At once, we began to write out the article for the newspaper. As I wrote, he translated. Antoine sat at the other end of the table, pale and sardonic.

"We must have a little introduction, something about "the well-known English poet, Elizabeth Greatorex, speaking with our special correspondent, said—'"

"She isn't a well-known poet." Antoine could not resist it.

"You would not know. You don't read my poems."

"He has not read one of them" I said, turning to Klaus. Klaus's head shot up, and his face stiffened. Slowly, he drawled: "Oh, I see."

Antoine was grinning; a wide smile.

"Why are you always laughing? You never do anything but grin."

The smile left Antoine's face.

I tried to write a few more lines, but the tension in the room made it impossible.

"For heaven's sake, go and get things settled at the Reisebureau, while I finish this article."

By the time they came back, the article was finished, and Klaus was just able to finish the translation before he went away.

We crossed the road to fetch his luggage.

Herr Hartmann put on his spectacles to read the article; it seemed to please him. It is to appear in next Tuesday's edition. Frau Hartmann gave me a photograph of one of her husband's wood carvings: a goblin-like man and dog. The carving resembled the carver, who is small and humped and beak-nosed. Frau Hartmann, who is his second wife, comes from Hamburg. She has an eye for men, and is enchanted by Antoine and Klaus. This morning, she stood arm in arm with Klaus, trying to flirt with him: "Ah, Herr Doktor."

At the bus stop, Klaus walked up and down with me. He talked nonsense with a forced gaiety, staying close to me until the last moment. I kissed him; it was the first time I had done so. Afterwards, I was afraid that my action might have embarrassed or offended him. The expression his face wears at home came back when he waved goodbye.

I rested after lunch. Antoine sat in the living-room with Frau Schmidt, who seemed to have recovered from her disappointment at being refused permission to visit the Russian zone. With peasant doggedness, she was making a garment for her granddaughter.

I should like to sleep for ever now that Klaus has gone away.

We dined at the Bahnhof, and quarrelled bitterly. My resentment at Antoine's childish behaviour having been suppressed during the past seven days, it now broke out.

Nightlong, I slide and slip and fall; on snowslopes and in imperious forests, looking for Klaus in my dreams.

> *Tout aussitot que je commence à prendre*
> *Dans le mol lit le repos désiré,*
> *Mon triste esprit hors de moy retiré*
> *S'en va vers toy incontinent se rendre.*

THIS morning, Frau Hartmann asked us to take coffee with her one day this week.

Fraülein Prass has gone away. We miss her; it is now dull at the family table, without laughter; only solemn card-playing every night. The young policeman still comes, but the other suitor has deserted the Bahnhof.

It rained today, and there was dense fog. Neither of us had the heart to ski in such weather: besides, we were both depressed, so we spent the morning in the warm Bahnhof, drinking coffee. I took my day-book along, and brought my notes up to date.

Against the bark-shingled gable of the house across the road, drooped a snowy fir tree. In the room where we sat, between the double windows, was a hyacinth covered with white flowers. In another window stood a pot of orange and yellow parrot tulips in a green pot.

By this morning's post there was already a letter from Klaus, written and posted in Goslar while he was waiting for his train. He had taken our ski-map by mistake, and now returned it with a letter illustrated by a drawing of Antoine and me, surrounded by phantom trees like those on the Rehberg.

"I think the sun was glad to see us, and that must have been why he came out of the clouds to visit us," he wrote. "I forgot to give you the map. Perhaps you won't be able to find the tracks and you will stand in the forest for a whole week with snow falling on your heads and shoulders. Here is the map. With it, perhaps you will be able to find the trails without your guide."

In the evening, we went for a walk past the Bowl, the Hubertus Hütte, and along the road towards the sanatorium. The sky had cleared, and the rain had turned to a delicate rime on the trees. There was a half moon and one bright star. It put me in mind of one of Flaubert's letters to Louise Colet, written at midnight; the one that begins: "The sky is clear; the moon is shining... Are you asleep, I wonder? Are you at the window? Are you thinking of one who thinks of you? Are you dreaming? What is the colour of your dream?"

JANUARY 20

IT froze hard during the night, giving icy conditions. We went up the Bruckberg once more, in pale sunshine. On our way down, it was still icy; for once, I was glad not to have steel edges to my skis, as, without them, my speed was just controllable. Antoine, with steel edges and a faster wax, found his speed almost impossible to control.

Today, lacerated faces have appeared. Men look as though they have been slashed with fine whips. On the way home, the slopes of the Rehberg gave very fast skiing. It was now imperative not to fall, after seeing the faces of those who had had the misfortune to hit the surface.

The quarrel continues, regarding my relationship to Klaus. Antoine repeats, over and over: "Why did you not tell me before about yourself and that man?"

It is useless to protest the truth, that up to now there has been nothing to tell.

Nothing can ever transcend the joy of last week; the despair of the present.

Elko's mother had her birthday today. She sent Elko up to us with a dish of cakes. Frau Schmidt sent him downstairs for photographs of his father. These contained a snapshot of his father and mother, inscribed to "my darling".

JANUARY 21

A FRESH snowfall has masked the ice, but the surface is so furrowed with ski marks that it is difficult to find one's way through this old spoor. It is like running in tramlines, with points to cross or jump. The hillside from the hunting lodge to the sanatorium has become our favourite run. This afternoon, we were the only ones out there. The fog was so thick that we lost each other at the distance of only a few yards. There was an absolute hush: not even the creaking of a branch from the black depth of trees. A stag called, and a dog barked. There was a faint clash of sleigh bells. The foliage was so frosted, it hung limp as if heavy with Spanish moss.

It was visiting day at the sanatorium. Our skis rushed us to the road running past the sterile buildings. When we go by I have a deep sense of guilt. I cough involuntarily, and stifle it because it increases the guilt-feeling. Voices echo from the open corridors, patients lean on balconies watching us. I try to hurry away from the accusing eyes.

On the drive, coming away from the sanatorium, is a black-coated woman, and a child carrying a doll. The child is chattering happily; the woman does not answer.

Our table at the Bahnhof was occupied tonight, so we sat in the other corner under the picture of *Napoleon In Exile*. Herr Prass shrugged his shoulders helplessly at us, and seemed to be quite upset about our table being occupied. Antoine, who had been looking past me at the opposite wall, said: "Look behind you." My article had been framed, and was hanging over our table.

The timid little suitor (in my romance of the daughter of the Bahnhof) we discovered sitting alone in Hotel Bergmann, looking more dejected than ever. I suppose he cannot bear to go to the Bahnhof now that she is no longer there.

Antoine and I have enjoyed an easy relationship for six years. Until now, I did not realize how shallow is the foundation of our life together.

Fräulein Stork came upstairs and demanded of us, "The book, the book." I could not think what she meant. "The English book with words."

"Ah, the lexicon."

Frau Schmidt winked bawdily, and gave a sentimental sigh.

"She wants to write to England, to Elko's pappi," she said.

JANUARY 22

I LIKE to watch the village life. There are the horse-drawn sledges, bell-ringing their way past lorries filled with snow; and children pass, taking babies out for an airing, in cradles fixed on sledges. A Russian troika, splendidly painted and with carved serpents' heads as decoration, goes by, drawn by two black horses. A bus passes, on its way to Goslar.

Of the Schäferhof, I do not yet dare to think.

Last night, under the surveillance of the clock, I lay awake, thinking of the eventual return to the island; my mind full of dread. I remember with aversion the sour, wet fields; the neighbourless, friendless sea-rock. This has been so happy a time.

Klaus has again written to us, giving the time at which our train is due to arrive at Löhne. Helga has written too, in a friendly mood, saying she looks forward to our return and that she loves us both.

A third note has come from Klaus, asking us to pick up his slippers left behind at Frau Hartmann's. We collected them this morning. The woman laughed about Herr Doktor, and the enormous amounts of snow he always brought into the house on his boots.

This afternoon we went to take coffee with her. She was scarcely the same woman. Her face was grey; her eyes heavily shadowed. She explained in whispers that her husband had been taken seriously ill, very suddenly, and he was now in a high fever. After a whispered conversation, we left.

JANUARY 23

SINCE it is our last day of skiing, we have spent the time on Matthias Schmidt Berg. I have found the courage to come down the mountain by one of the more difficult ways. Klaus had left a number of ski-lift tickets with us; we used them today.

ELKO had been waiting for hours to take our gear to the bus-stop on his sled. It was snowing heavily through the fog-blanket; the air was intensely dry and hard.

I discovered, in a shop in a side street, a book I have been trying to obtain for a long time: Rainer Maria Rilke's *Die Weise von Liebe und Tod des Cornets Christoph Rilke*, in the Insel-Bücherei edition.

Last night, we ordered an early lunch for today, in the Bahnhof. We are sitting now, waiting for it to be served. I open the book:

> *Reiten, reiten, reiten, durch den Tag, durch die Nacht,*
> *durch den Tag.*
> *Reiten, reiten, reiten.*
> *... Ist das der Morgen? Welche Sonne geht auf?*
> *Wie groß ist die Sonne? Sind das Vögel?*
> *Ihre Stimmen sind überall.*

As keepsakes, Herr Prass gave us two wine glasses, carefully packed in a cigar box.

"Goodbye, goodbye." Herr Ober bowed us out for the last time.

At noon, Frau Schmidt and Elko saw us off. The fog was dense as far as Sonnenberg, and beyond. Trees and branches lay broken in a part of the forest that skirted the road. Overhead, telegraph wires covered in ice and snow hung in loops. Below Altenau the earth was dingy. After three weeks spent in a white world, it was a surprise to see the soft green of moss on the banks, and the cool grey of rock.

In Goslar, it was damp and terribly cold. We waited for our train in the impersonal Bahnhof in the ordinary town. I longed for the mysterious hush of Sankt Andreasberg. Was it at this table, Klaus wrote his letter to me last Sunday?

The train carried us to Löhne. I saw him at the other end of the subway: he had his back to us.

Albrecht and the cart were in the station yard. Antoine lifted me up onto the driving seat. Klaus put the carriage-lamp into my hand, and climbed up beside me. Antoine sat behind us, in the basket chair.

I found it difficult to plumb Klaus's mood. He was not the same person who had been with us in the mountains. He looked so tired and tense that I thought perhaps he was sorry to see us again. He seemed to have aged in a week. My high spirits had returned as soon as I saw his broad back in the fur-collared coat but, sitting beside him in the cart, I tried to sense what had happened to change him. He sat hunched forward, barely watching the road. In the faint light from the stars, he kept searching my face. His spectacles gave him an almost owlish absorption. Antoine said nothing, but his presence was like a shout.

Klaus spoke a little, spasmodically.

"It is nice to see you again…"

"It is lovely to see you, too. Oh, I must tell you; I went straight down the mountain yesterday, several times. On the last run, I landed on the side of my head, at the bottom of a steep snow-wall. I did not even suffer from a headache."

"A lot of things have happened this week."

"What has happened?"

"The kitchen ceiling fell down just after Opa and Oma had gone away."

"Gracious! What did you do about it?"

"It is replastered. A workman and I did it together. It was only finished this evening."

"How tired you must be. I wish now that you had not come to meet us."

"No, I wanted to come. It is nice to be in the cart after being indoors all day... Another thing, very funny, happened last night. I was taking a load of vegetables to the Obernburg. Something frightened Albrecht, and he turned the cart over into a field; me and the vegetables, everything. My hat fell off into the road. Cars went over it. I thought, 'Oh, oh, what will Helga say if the hat is spoilt?' Two men came to pick me up. They stared at me, and then at one another. They said, 'See here, aren't you the man we picked up out of a field a month ago?' I replied, 'Yes, I suppose so. Albrecht often does this sort of thing.'"

"Did you get your hat from the road?" I asked.

"Yes... The cart was a little damaged."

Now I understood why the floor in front of the seat felt insecure.

From time to time, heavy traffic passed us. When I heard an approaching vehicle, I held out the lamps as far as possible. Once, when a heavy lorry failed to see our light, it was only by drawing the cart against the wall of a house that my friend saved us from accident.

A watery moon sped through high ragged cloud. Klaus was watching me. "The moon is still there," he said.

"How is Helga? How are the children?"

"They are well. They have gone to the Obernburg."

"Will they be back tonight?"

"They have gone for a few days; Anni is with them."

"When did they go?"

"They went away on Wednesday."

"Who is with you at the Schäferhof?"

"I am alone. Now, you will be there."

I should have been delighted by this situation, for it would give me an opportunity to be alone with him; but because I had not dreamed of such an event, I was taken unawares, and found myself dismayed. Helga must have gone to the Obernburg because she does not want to see me again.

The Schäferhof was in darkness, so Klaus went into the stable to unlock the house door from the inside.

The house was dirty and thick with dust. Under the hall mirror stood my pot of cyclamen. It had grown long, pale, and dejected; the flowers were withered brown.

Between us, we made supper. I stood over the gas stove, cooking fish, with no sense of reality.

"Antoine, you will sleep here tonight. There is no need for you to go to the other farm. You and Elizabeth can have my bedroom. I shall sleep in the other room."

The only feeling I have tonight is one of anti-climax, a falling-away from the mountain tops.

116

3

TIDAL WAVE

WHEN I went into Klaus's room to make his bed, I found on the table by the window the photograph of Brita whose absence from the other bedroom I had noticed last night. Why did he remove it from his and Helga's bedroom; and why should the picture of Helga's dead brother be now turned face to the wall?

In the yard is another sign of a quarrel having taken place; a pair of women's size gumboots, thrown among the straw and filth. I can imagine Helga throwing them out in a rage, before she left for the luxury of the Obernburg.

After the past-haunted forests, and the white frost-flowers, I cannot bear to look at this blind countryside. No snow lies here; the ground is hard with bitterness, the surface is wet and slimy as the earth of a graveyard.

Johannes and Sidi, with two of their children, Kornelius and Inser, arriving unexpectedly from Schwarzenmoor, were delighted to see us looking so fit and brown. Klaus brought out the *Zeitung*, and showed them the article on Andreasberg.

They seemed no more than mildly surprised at finding that Helga and the children were away from home. Kornelius went into the nursery as if he expected to find them hiding under the furniture.

Inser has lost her shyness with me, and now sits close, chattering in broken English.

Before they left, Sidi said: "Elizabeth, I want you to come to see us. Will Tuesday be suitable?"

Klaus and Antoine went to buy cakes at the shop down the road, and to phone Kurt and Selma, asking them to come over to coffee. There is no mention of Helga's return, or of our going to see her.

There are no servants in the house, so the stoves have been left to go out. It is now so intensely cold that the men have lit fires in the kitchen, the living-room, and the bedroom. At first, the kitchen fire would not burn, so they brought in an iron pot containing benzine and poured it onto the smouldering wood in the stove. There was a burst of flame; the benzine in the pot caught fire; hastily, they lowered the pot to the wooden floor. Smoke and flames poured out until the air was thick with blue smoke. We looked apprehensively at the newly-plastered ceiling. Antoine rushed outside, and returned with a big iron lid with which he smothered the flames. Klaus did nothing to put out the fire, but shouted and laughed like a schoolboy.

The house has taken on a different atmosphere: one of almost feverish festivity; it has a much more hopeful air, though it still smells of babies and cats and poor shivering Yula.

In the early afternoon, while we were resting after lunch, I could hear Klaus moving about downstairs. The living-room was quite transformed when I went down. He had put a clean cloth on the table, drawn a curtain across the gas stove, swept the floor, and placed cups and saucers and a mound of cakes on the table.

The three of us sat upstairs waiting for the guests. Before they arrived, Yula barked. Anni's sister stood at the door, with a message from the Obernburg.

An hour later, Yula barked again. Through the branches of the fruit trees, we could see Kurt and Selma walking across the field.

It was a happy reunion, with everyone in tearing spirits. The Hastfers wanted to hear our adventures.

Selma noticed the gumboots lying on the dungheap.

"Look," she laughed. "Whose are those?"

"Helga's," said Klaus stiffly.

After coffee, the five of us sat upstairs talking about Andreasberg. What a different reception Selma has had today in this room, unlike the last time I saw her here; the night before we left for the mountains.

They spoke of the illness of Klaus's mother and stepfather.

"Poor things, they lie there side by side. They are both very ill," said Selma. Turning to me, she said: "Did you know that Herr von Ravenstadt never comes here? He came once, when we were getting the house ready for Helga before the marriage. He only came as far as the door; took one look inside, and fled home across the fields."

At dusk, to Antoine's and my surprise, Oma and Opa arrived. I think Oma is glad to be back, though she has plenty to praise in her new home. Opa is not staying the night; he only came to be company for Oma in the dark. He says little, but he misses nothing; staring round with hard black eyes behind thick lenses.

After the arrival of the old people, a sense of oppression came over me. Something serious must have happened to cause Klaus to send for Oma. Am I in any way responsible for the quarrel?

Klaus and Selma went downstairs to prepare supper.

Opa broke silence to ask Kurt, "Why did Frau von Dorn run away?"

"She did not run away. Klaus took her to the Obernburg."

I went downstairs, and said: "Klaus, are you unhappy?" I took it for granted that he must be unhappy without his wife and babies. He was uncorking a bottle of wine, and gave a loud shout at my question, laughed, and said: "No, I am happy."

After supper, talking of the island, I spoke of the occasional hardship of life there. He leaned forward, listening, with tears in his eyes.

"It is not romantic to live on an island. The romance lies in the idea. My friends like to think of me there, it appeals to them, and they feel they have me pinned down. They know where I am."

"It is the same with me," put in Klaus. "My friends think it is romantic that I am here on the farm with the babies."

Antoine tells me that while I was downstairs, Opa said to Kurt, "Klaus is a bad man."

"No," returned Kurt. "He is a good man."

Selma has asked us to go to them on Thursday. Klaus is to take over a supply of vegetables, and we are to arrive for lunch. Selma is going to make a special Polish dish in our honour.

JANUARY 26

I SHOULD like to go away today or tomorrow. I have told Klaus of my intention: he thinks I am joking, and insists that we stay until after next weekend. I said I could not bear to feel that Helga had gone away because we were here: if we went, would she not come home?

He replied that she went because she was tired after the work on the kitchen ceiling; and tired of the inconvenience of not having running water. He assured me that Helga had nothing but friendly feelings for me. It was pleasant for him, he said, to have us, now that he was alone.

From something he said yesterday to Opa, the disagreement with Helga took place on Saturday morning, the day of our return; but I must not take it too seriously. I have to laugh at Antoine's distorted idea of the wicked count! For he has got it fixed firmly in his mind that Klaus sent Helga away so that he could have me to himself.

JANUARY 27

A WET, cold, dark morning. We had some time to wait in Herford for the bus to Schwarzenmoor, so Klaus went into the town to buy wine and flowers. He bought two bunches of sweet-scented violets, one for Sidi, and one for me.

In the Schwarzenmoor living-room, the blond young man we had seen at Christmas was sitting by the stove with his head in his hands. At sight of us, he jumped up and went into the yard.

After lunch, when the children had come home from school, Inser showed me her exercise books, and talked about her dog and her father's horses.

"You do my English exercise for me, while I play," she said.

The children displayed an embarrassing curiosity about Helga's absence.

"Uncle Klaus, you are a hard-boiled bachelor," said Inser. "How are you able to get on now that aunt Helga is not there?"

"Elizabeth is with me."

"Oma is doing the cooking," I put in.

Klaus insisted that I should have an hour's rest. He took me upstairs, and covered me with a warm rug on Inser's bed.

Wind besieges the house. It has scarcely become light all day; rain gushes down the windows, but I am still safe in Klaus's love for another few days.

When I awoke, Inser was in the room. "Here is my dog. Do you like her, Elizabeth? Did you have a good rest? It is coffee-time."

The living-room was fragrant with the scent of Klaus's violets. At tea, Antoine told of Frau Schmidt's joke; of how she said I should return alone to England, while Antoine stayed with her. They would marry and she would give him a farm.

"Antoine could stay in the Harz. Uncle Klaus could go to England with Elizabeth." A dead silence followed Inser's words.

There was a knock at the door, and the blond young man came in. Johannes and he had a low-voiced conversation; then Johannes went over to his desk and wrote on a paper which he gave to the young man.

Sidi explained. "His old trouble has come back," she said. "He must go away for shock treatment. His brother committed suicide; and he himself has been in a mental hospital since the war."

"Was it as a result of being a prisoner?"

"No, it is in his family. He comes of a good family, but there is a taint."

We had thought of leaving after coffee, to see the film of *Don Camillo and Peppone* in Herford, of which everyone is speaking; but Sidi said she would be pleased for us to stay until after supper.

With the exception of Johannes, the family is temperamental. The children scream and rage; Sidi shrieks at them, but Johannes remains calm and aloof.

The scent of violets!

Sidi started a discussion on the place of the woman in the home and in society. She is profoundly dissatisfied with her life. She has to work hard in this large house; with her family and outdoor servants to feed. She would like to do anything but endless housework. I asked her what she would like to do.

"Interior decorating."

"Why don't you start on this house, then?" asked Klaus. "There is plenty of scope for you here."

"No," she said, looking round at the oak-panelled room. "This house does not interest me."

"Antoine hates me to go away, even when it is in connection with my work," I said. "He cannot bear to be alone on the island and when I come back, he is angry because I have been away."

"That is bad," said Klaus.

"What would you do if your wife had a career that took her away from home?"

"I should be pleased for her to go away for her work. When she came back, I should give her a big welcome."

Johannes took no part in our conversation. He watched Sidi with amused alarm, as if he had discovered a new person in her. His only interest is in the land and in different makes of tractor.

Sidi suddenly became savage.

"What we want is internationalism, not nationalism; and true freedom for women... It is terrible, always to be in fear. I am afraid, increasingly afraid, for Inser. She is only thirteen years of age, but already, she is very tall for her years. If the Russians came, she would be noticed at once, and taken to Siberia. Perhaps this year, or maybe next year, Russia will overrun the west zone as she overran the east. The whole of Europe will become her colony."

Turning to Johannes, she said: "I beg of you, let us leave this farm and go to a small house. Only give me a garden, somewhere to grow fruit and vegetables. In that way, we shall not starve when the enemy comes. Nobody would notice us if we lived so modestly."

Inser had gone out into the wild dark night, to exercise her dog. She had been away a long time. Before Sidi mentioned Siberia, it had seemed safe for her to be out alone; now, I imagined all manner of dangers in wait for the tall girl in the dark avenue of Schwarzenmoor. Sidi grew nervous, too. She asked me to go to the outer door and to call the child.

It was a dark world. The wind roared in the trees. I remembered the story of the Polish servants waiting to kill their new German masters.

"Inser! Inser!"

She came in, about an hour later; fresh and animated as

126

she always is. Proudly, she showed me the waterproof she puts on her dog for winter walks.

After supper, Johannes took us in his car to Herford for the last bus to Löhne. Just before we left, Sidi said: "If you would like it, Inser can come to the Schäferhof for the weekend. She could come straight after school on Saturday."

JANUARY 28

THE weather grows worse each day. The wind has been rising since Sunday, and it rains intermittently.

Oma discovered the gumboots in the yard.

"Whose are those?"

"My wife's."

She clicked her tongue, picked the boots out of the straw and cow-dung, and washed them under the kitchen pump. They now stand with the other boots and clogs in the hall.

During the morning, I could find neither Klaus nor Antoine. While I was standing at the front door, wondering where they could be, Opa came out of the house. He is here again, back at his old job of chopping firewood and feeding the cows. He seized my arm, muttering about 'the young men', but I could not make out what he was talking about. I should like to pull his spectacles off; to see what his eyes are like, whether he is really as blind as he appears to be.

When the men came in from the eternal task of picking sprouts, I told Klaus of how Opa had seized my arm.

He laughed. "You must be careful of Opa. He is a wicked old man. When we had a dance here, Opa wanted to dance

127

with the prettiest girls, but Oma soon settled that: she made him go and sit with her in the kitchen. She keeps a strict eye on him. Opa, if Oma had not taken him away, would have outdanced the young men."

In the middle of lunch, one of the Obernburg maid-servants arrived with a letter for Klaus from Helga. I did not dare to look at his face; I knew it must be wearing the expression I had grown to dread, a set look with the eyes out of focus.

Having read the letter, he sat staring before him. Later, he went upstairs to write an answer. The girl took the letter and set off over the fields on her bicycle. Almost immediately afterwards, Klaus set out in the same direction in the cart.

"I am going to the mill. On the way back, I shall get the saddle so that you can ride Albrecht tonight. I shall be home by coffee-time."

I guessed that Helga had sent for him to come to the Obernburg and that she intends to come home sometime today.

I could not bear to stay any longer in the house, waiting for him to return. Even Oma is depressed; she is as puzzled as we are.

"Shall we go for a walk?" suggested Antoine.

The roads were covered in a sticky mud; the countryside was flat and mournful. Schoolboys in peaked caps stopped their games to see us go by. We walked round onto the road towards the main Schäferhof, and then went in the direction of the Obernburg. I was afraid of our meeting the returning cart.

Some time after we were back at the farm, I looked out of the window, to see Klaus's figure, alone in the cart, coming round the corner beside the wood. I ran down the stairs to greet him as he came into the house. He threw down a heavy cavalry saddle, looked up at me where I stood on the stairs, and said: "There you are. Now you can ride Albrecht this evening, as soon as we have had coffee."

He was once more in good spirits. "Helga sent you her love. She is coming back tonight."

"How will she come?"

"The chauffeur from the Obernburg will bring her. Sophie has gone to Winterberg for the day; but as soon as she comes back, the car will be free for Helga."

I felt that without an explanation from Klaus before his wife arrived, I would not be able to face her.

During coffee, he noticed my silence. "Are you thinking about a poem, or are you sad?"

I shook my head, without replying. Antoine was watching me, but he kept silent.

"Now! You ride. I will put the saddle on Albrecht." He rushed away to the stable.

"Antoine, I must have an explanation from him. I cannot bear this mystery! I am going to speak with him upstairs."

"Better to get it cleared up."

I met him in the hall. "Klaus, I must talk with you. Can we go upstairs?"

He followed without a word, and we sat down in the bedroom. After switching on the wall lamp, he whispered: "What is the matter?"

"It is not to be borne... I understand nothing. First of all, Helga goes away, just before our return; you send for Oma. Now, you say Helga is coming home. You say it as if nothing had happened. How can I meet her?"

"There is nothing to worry about. We had a quarrel, a little one, nothing; about a litre of milk. Besides, she was tired and thought it would be better to go to the Obernburg where she could have a rest."

"She wrote to us in the mountains, as if she wanted to see us again."

"So she did. She was looking forward to your return. Then, at the last moment, she decided to go. We did have a quarrel, but it is settled now. I went to the Obernburg this afternoon, and took her and the children for a drive on the road. In her letter, she asked for you to come over also, but I told her you were tired and needed a rest. She is coming here to see you instead, tonight. She wanted to get away from here, to be alone. Now, she says she is lonely... nobody visits her. She cannot sleep."

"Are you sure she has no hard feelings towards me?"

"No. You are too sensitive."

"I cannot bear to see you unhappy. You often quarrel, don't you?"

"Yes: it is difficult for a man and woman to live together."

I told him: "After you left St. Andreasberg, it was terrible. Antoine and I quarrelled every day; he is so jealous of you. It was unbearable without you."

"A week is a short time."

"Antoine said you had done wrong to take an extra day with us. He found fault, even with that."

"No, it was not wrong. It was one day when we could be together. Helga has all the rest of the year to be nice to me if she pleases..."

I thought of how she has the rest of their lifetime together.

130

"Helga has no peace in herself. I cannot..." he hesitated.

"It is not my fault, but I cannot get close to her. I have tried, but she makes shallow conversation."

"It is the same with me. I am her husband, and cannot be close to her."

"The night Selma brought me back from the Obernburg, it was terrible."

"How dreadful it was, that night. She does not like friends to come to the house, yet she always says she is lonely; and would like me to take her visiting the dentist's wife and the doctor's wife in Herford."

Outside, the storm was increasing with the darkness. The trees scratched at the window. Owing to the high wind, the electric light faded out. We sat in silence, side by side, until it came slowly on again.

"She seems to like people when she meets them for the first time. After a while, she becomes bored. Isn't that how it is?"

"Yes... When I came home from the mountains, she was not angry because I had stayed an extra day, but because I had forgotten to give her my address. Always, when I have been away, she picks on some small thing to bring against me."

"Forgive me: do you love her?"

"Not as I loved Brita. She says I am cold, that I don't love her; that I'm still always thinking of Brita."

We were seated close together on the bed. The furrow down his brow, the lines on his cheeks, were deep with the pain of his thoughts. I raised my left hand and stroked his cheek.

"You are not cold."

His eyes remained fixed on the wall.

"My dear; listen to me. There is something I must tell you. I wanted to say it in Andreasberg. I love you very much."

"Oh." He turned swiftly round to face me. His arms went round me, so that I was sheltered against the cage of his ribs.

"We loved one another for twenty years," he said softly, "but there is much water between us. Why did you want to leave here the other day? Is it because I cannot make it nice enough for you on the Schäferhof? I thought it would be lovely to have you here alone for a week."

"I am too much alone on the island."

"But you have Antoine."

"I am not happy there."

"Is he cruel to you?" he questioned.

"No, no." I had to laugh. "Antoine is good and kind, not cruel. Only, now he is jealous, it makes him behave stupidly."

"I don't know what it is to be jealous. It must be terrible."

"He wants to imprison me in his love."

"How wrong that is of him. Love, flying over the hills and over the sea to the sun and stars, is like an angel coming from the good Lord; like a bird singing in the trees, like the wind in springtime. Elizabeth, think of me in the spring, when I walk behind the plough, with Albrecht stamping the earth and blowing his breath into the cold morning."

"I love you."

"It is wonderful to be loved."

"Helga tried to speak against you to me but I would not listen."

"You should have listened to her. Perhaps I am very bad, and perhaps it is good that you are going far away from me. Oh my dear, don't be dragged two ways. Stay close to Antoine whom you know to be a good man. Let me go with you in your poetry, this most difficult way, but don't forget the other way with your husband. I like him, and I think he is your counterpoint, and you would be unhappy without him."

"It will be difficult because we are so different."

"Often, it is difficult to live with a man whose soul is different…. Let us be good friends, and we shall be closer together than lovers."

"The wind is rising. The sea will he rough tonight."

"The next war may kill us off; then it will be good to remember one another in our last moments."

"England, when I return, will be a foreign country. London will be a desert."

"Remember your best friend in the desert of London, in that foreign country."

"Listen! The trees are roaring like the sea at high water."

"Perhaps, when you get home, you will sit on a rock, my little mermaid, and will look out over the ocean. It isn't easy to be happy with what we have. When Gottfried has a book, Angelika wants it, because it seems better than her own toys. So children begin, and old people end. Dry your tears, and smile at me." Very gently, he began to stroke my hands.

"If I can get reliable peasants to work here after Oma and Opa have left, I shall try to visit you on your island during the summer."

"You would love everything: the birds and the seals singing day and night in summertime. The flowers!"

"I forgot to tell you, Helga will be here just after dinner."

"What is the time?" I asked. "Antoine must be wondering what is the matter, but I told him I must speak with you."

Oma shouted at the stairfoot, "Herr von Dorn, it is dinner-time."

"Very well, we are coming."

As I moved towards the door, Klaus followed me, and took me in his arms.

Antoine was in the living-room, with a book in his hands. His face was white. He leapt up at sight of us, saying fiercely:

"This is the end, the absolute end." He rushed upstairs.

I had come from the interview utterly at peace, ready to face Helga, and to be reconciled with Antoine.

"Klaus, what shall I do? Now, everything is worse than ever."

"Go after him, and bring him downstairs."

In the bedroom, Antoine stood at bay.

"Antoine, I have been speaking with Klaus to straighten things out before Helga comes back. Why do you behave like this?"

"You came downstairs, smiling happily, after being upstairs for two hours. I've walked round and round the wood. What do you think I have been feeling? Oma was upset; she kept coming in and asking where Klaus was."

"I told you I had to talk with him. Please come down to dinner."

Klaus had poured out schnapps for himself and for Antoine.

"No," said my husband, "I don't want to drink with you."

"Shall we go outside for a fight?"

"No." Antoine was sulky.

Towards the end of the meal, the outer door opened. Klaus said:

"Helga is here," and went out, closing the door.

"My God, what a household," said Antoine.

When Helga came in, we rose to greet her, and I gave her my place at the table. She was gracious, but distant in manner. She was wearing a thick white woollen shawl over her blue frock. As usual, she had the meal removed as soon as possible, and began immediately to prepare for bed. Antoine and I wanted her and Klaus to have their own bedroom; but she said no, we were not to disturb ourselves. She was only going to stay the night, and would be going on to Herford to see the doctor in the morning. We were coming to the Obernburg on Thursday to the Hastfers, were we not? We should see her then, and the children.

"Klaus, I must bring the babies home; I am afraid they will become ill with so much infection around them. I still cannot sleep. Diogenes, the Hastfers' dog, barks the whole night. Seven already have the grippe at the Obernburg."

It was an immense relief to go to bed, for Helga's coming had put the final constraint on us. After his wife's return, Klaus scarcely looked at me, and as for Antoine, he was pale and silent.

Helga had my old room, where her husband had been sleeping; and he slept on a small hard bed in the children's nursery.

I looked through his bookshelves before getting into bed. What an extraordinary chance! I found Sacheverell Sitwell's *The Homing of the Winds*; and in it this sentence:

"We wrote in communion with one another and mine will always be the freedom of her world."

Klaus might have written those words.

But my greatest consolation is John Donne. How fortunate it is that I should have a volume of his poems with me.

> Rend us in sunder, thou canst not divide
> Our bodies so, but that our souls are ty'd,
> And we can love by letters still and gifts,
> And thoughts and dreams;
>
> They who one another keep alive
> N'er parted be.

JANUARY 29

IMMEDIATELY after breakfast, while Helga was getting ready to go into the town, Klaus shouted: "Now, you must ride Albrecht."

Helga lent me a pair of her own riding boots, so large for me that there was danger of my losing them. Albrecht is a powerful beast of sixteen and a half hands. Antoine had to throw me up into the saddle. Yula went along, scampering through the puddles. When I said "Good morning" to a small boy with a satchel of school-books at his back, he glanced fearfully up at me, perched high above the clumsy legs of the great horse; but made no reply. A hollow-cheeked peasant woman was wading through mud and snow-sludge.

I trotted for about a mile, then turned the horse's head for home; whereupon he broke into a gallop. It was like being on a whale's back. The rough track was pitted with water-filled holes, over which the powerful beast bounded at full stride. Albrecht seemed to have forgotten my existence; he was having a private gallop for his own amusement. As we approached the road, I reined him in; he slowed down reluctantly, unwilling to remember that he was not free to take huge leaps over the land. We were passed by a bridal carriage drawn by two heavy geldings, and driven by a man in top hat and frock coat.

There was the sound of a church bell, being rung perhaps for the dead.

After changing my boots, I joined the men in the fields, and picked brussels sprouts until my fingers felt completely dead. A skin of ice covered each sprout and leaf.

Having prepared the vegetables for market, we put them in the cart and went to the Obernburg. Before going to Selma's apartment, Klaus took us for a few moments to Helga's rooms where we saw the babies, quite transformed from the little urchins they are at home. Gottfried's hair was shining silk.

Helga's sister was there, and Anni, who was plainly revelling in being a nursemaid at a castle. Helga was as vague and distrait as ever.

Klaus went back home in the cart, saying he would return at about seven o'clock. He and Opa had a plan to distemper the walls of the kitchen and bedrooms.

I rested as I had done before, in the drawing-room; slept, and awoke refreshed. Antoine and Kurt came in at coffee-time, bringing with them the materials for making Tar Tar, which we are to have for dinner.

Selma began her preparations. She cracked the eggs, being careful not to break the yolks; and chopped up onions very fine. Meat, consisting of the finest quality pounded raw beefsteak, was apportioned to each plate. Pepper, salt, and oil, were put on the table. Meanwhile, Kurt and Antoine were opening five bottles of wine to go into the punch bowl over a layer of peaches.

Klaus arrived in the early evening. In the hall, I saw the old Schäferhof rugs that were always used in the cart, and realized how important they had become to me.

Selma asked him: "What do you think? Shall we invite Helga to come up after dinner?"

He shrugged his shoulders in disdainful indifference; Selma rang down to Sophie's apartment and gave a message to Helga.

Each of us sat with a plateful of raw beefsteak. Kurt directed operations.

"Pound up the meat with your forks."

"Next: pepper, salt, oil."

"A little chopped onion."

"The raw egg; break it into the meat."

"Pepper, salt, oil."

"A little more onion."

"Turn the meat over; pound it."

The others were finished before I was halfway through mine. There was a tap at the door. Helga stood outside, wearing her white shawl, which gave her an elderly appearance. She showed diffidence; smiled, spoke a little, but was obviously unhappy. At sight of her, Klaus had become constrained also.

We went into the drawing-room.

"The punch! The punch!" cried Kurt.

"How hot it is in here," said Selma. She opened the double panes of one of the windows. "Look at the snow on the trees. How dark the water is!"

At ten o'clock Helga grew restless. She murmured that she must go to bed. Klaus took her to her apartment.

"Old Klaus and Helga, the love birds, have gone to look at the moonlight," laughed Kurt.

Selma gazed thoughtfully at the carpet. She leant towards me, saying softly: "Did you manage to speak with Klaus?"

"Yes."

"How was he in Sankt Andreasberg?"

"Happy, absolutely happy."

At that moment, Klaus came back. With a sigh, he relaxed on the divan beside Antoine.

He looked across at me: "Vivica wants to say good night to you," he said.

I went to the child in her fantasy-haunted room. She clung to me with feverish hands.

"Will you come to see me when you are older?" I asked her.

"Yes, yes. I will come with Mammi when I am fifteen years old."

I peeped into the grandmother's bedroom. "Godspeed on your homeward journey," said Selma's mother.

Over the punch, the men talked international politics in a mixture of tongues: German, English, French, and Latin.

139

At one-thirty in the morning, we began to get ready for the road. Diogenes barked loudly as we stumbled over the cobble-stones.

"Be quiet, Diogenes," warned Kurt.

"He will wake Helga—her room is just above," giggled Selma.

A thin rain was falling. It seemed a long way to the stableyard. The night felt like a blanket, something we must push aside in order to get safely home. Our small lantern was lit; by its feeble light, I could see Kurt and Selma, anxiously waving farewell.

"Antoine should hold the lantern. Elizabeth should sit behind."

"No, Elizabeth is to hold the lamp." With a rush, we were carried out onto the main road, only a small patch of which was illuminated by the lantern. Nonetheless, despite the feebleness of the light, Albrecht feared it, and the white steam rising from his own nostrils. He must also have seen goblins for several times he half swerved across the road to avoid objects which we could not see. When we came to the track onto the Schäferhof land, Klaus had to let him find his own way, for it was now impossible to make out either road or fields. It was after two o'clock when we bumped into the yard. The lights were on in the house and in the stable; the stable door stood open for the horse.

The photograph of Helga's brother is still turned to the wall, but the photograph of Brita has been for some time in its proper place. It was there when I went into the room on Sunday afternoon.

AFTER breakfast, I went riding. By the time I had reached the track where I galloped yesterday, it had come on to rain, which fell more and more heavily, forcing me to turn back to the farm. I was streaming water like a fish before I regained the Schäferhof.

Oma was in great distress this afternoon. She and Opa have been reported to the authorities as having rooms in two farms. All this arose because Klaus sent for them to come back temporarily last Sunday. Opa is afraid that he and Oma will find themselves without a roof over their heads. After a long conversation with Klaus and a visit to Löhne to put matters straight, he is today moving the last of his belongings to the new home.

It rains, it blows, it is horribly cold. The old people's few possessions – a battered chair, a rough bedstead, a bundle of bedclothes – were put into the farm wagon commonly used for carrying vegetables. Last of all, Opa staggered out with a huge crock of salted pork; then the old man led the horse and cart away through the mud and rain.

I have begun to pack my clothes, as we expect to leave here next Monday. Two of my sweaters, spoilt by snow at Sankt Andreasberg, I put out in the kitchen to be used as floor cloths. When I went for boiling water to make coffee, I found Oma standing by the table, her face radiant. She had never shown much feeling towards me before. She pointed to the old sweaters which now hung airing on the rack above the stove.

"They are for me? Can I have them?" she asked eagerly.

"But yes, of course you may have them if they are of any use to you."

She put her arms round my neck, and kissed me on both cheeks. She told me about her daughter's children in the Russian zone, for whom she would send the jerseys.

"In the east zone, they are hungry. They have almost no fats, and no potatoes."

In the evening, Klaus read aloud to me, translating as he went along, Rilke's *Liebe und Tod des Cornets Christoph Rilke*.

> *Es bäumt sich ein Leib*
> *den Baum entlang, und ein junges Weib,*
> *blutig und bloß,*
> *fällt ihn an: Mach mich los!*

JANUARY 31

A COLOSSAL wind rages over the land, carrying rain and sleet. Under the trees, small patches of snow resemble white birds.

"Look," said Antoine. "Aren't they like seagulls sheltering from a storm?"

Despite the weather, Klaus announced his intention of taking us to call on friends in Herford. I had understood that Inser was coming this afternoon for the weekend; but as Klaus did not mention it, I thought perhaps she was not coming after all.

We put on our best clothes, and picked our way across the field and through the sodden wood. Klaus was wearing gum-boots; before we came to the road, he went into a shed at the big Schäferhof to change into his yellow shoes.

Wind, confined in the narrow streets, roared through the town, tearing at placards, and flinging heavy signboards back and fore on rusty hinges.

We were in a side street, when Antoine said to me: "Don't look in that window."

I stopped instinctively, and saw displayed a peasant apron of a bright blue cotton. The square bib was covered in white, yellow, and black embroidery, as was also a wide band round the hem.

"Would you like it?" asked Klaus.

"It is beautiful, but it must be expensive. Please, no; I do not want it."

"We can ask the price," he declared, and took me into the shop, where I tried on the apron.

"It is just right for you," pronounced Klaus. He bought it and put it carefully away in his rucksack. Outside the shop, he took my arm. "It is for you to remember your visit by."

"I shall wear it on the island. When you come, I shall put it on for you."

The Eichendorffs, Klaus's friends, lived in a new house outside the town. After repeated knocking, the door was opened and a large head with grizzled hair peered cautiously out. It was Herr Eichendorff. He and his wife had been taking their siesta; he had on an overcoat which disclosed bare legs. He took us upstairs to an immaculate sitting-room, and called his wife.

Herr Eichendorff is an amateur anthropologist; he was a refugee landowner from the east zone. Nothing could offer a greater contrast than between Klaus and his friend, between Helga and Frau Eichendorff, between the Schäferhof and this spotless house. Eichendorff is a well-built man with a high-pitched voice. He is precise in his movements. His wife is a charming woman, who speaks a little English and perfect French. She was wearing a severe black velvet dress. Eichendorff showed us hundreds of reproductions, cave drawings, photographs of animals and birds. His enthusiasm was enormous, but too intense to be borne for long. In the course of a dissertation on racial characteristics, he said:

"Dark men have white souls. Blond men have black devils inside them."

After coffee, the inevitable album came out. How many of these have we now looked at? The mansion or castle, the park, the pedigree herd of cattle, the brood mare; the smiling group before the elegant shining motor car. We are invited into the past, to meet the dead or exiled. The castles have become tenements. The cattle, horses, cars, have vanished.

Eichendorff now teaches in a school in Herford.

By late evening, the gale reached its height. At about ten o'clock we left the house, within a short time of the last bus for Löhne for which we ran half-blinded by wet sticky snow.

We had not needed to hurry, for the bus, owing to the storm, was very late. Snow swirled by, driven on the furious wind. We took shelter in a doorway. I stood on the inside, within the porch, sheltered by the two men. Klaus seemed to tower, putting his bulk between me and the weather.

144

"When we get out of the bus, I shall carry you through the wood," he said.

There was only standing room in the vehicle. I was near the front, and was able to look through the driver's window. The snow, whose flakes were like silver-fish, rushed at the glass, were pushed aside by it, and whirled past. There were a few walkers on the road, with heads down, fighting their way into the storm.

Alighting from the bus, we stumbled into the entrance of the wood. Klaus disappeared: he had gone into the shed to change his shoes. I wanted to wait for him, but Antoine insisted that we should go on. We struggled through an immense confusion and fury of sound. Overhead, the trees roared. The air was choking with snow.

"I cannot go on. Where is Klaus? We should have waited for him."

Antoine seized me, and began to carry me along. I struggled against him, filled with panic terrors.

"Klaus! Klaus! Where are you?"

One moment he was not there, and the next, he was plunging strongly from the screaming tunnel of trees into the open field.

When he came up, he stared at me strangely, as if he had thought me lost. "There you are. I was going to carry you in the wood."

The house was full of lights. To our surprise, when we went into the living-room, we found Inser lying on the couch, reading a book.

Klaus was astonished: he had forgotten about her coming for the weekend.

"When did you arrive?"

"I came straight from school. I got here at half-past two. I have come to spend the weekend with you, Uncle Klaus."

So the house is full again. Klaus is sleeping in the children's room, Inser in the living-room, Oma in the bedroom next to ours.

FEBRUARY 1

THE inner casement of the living-room had been opened, and the curtains drawn back, but only to disclose a hostile world. A short time after the rising of a watery sun, the snow had melted into the earth. It became another wet day with the same high wind.

We were expected at the Obernburg today to say goodbye, but Klaus declared the weather was too bad for us to go. So we stayed quietly at home.

According to the newspapers, there was a phenomenal gale in the North Sea last night. More than one-sixth of Holland, the south-east coast of England, part of Belgium, have been inundated without warning; and the floods are still rising. In the north Irish Sea, a passenger ship has sunk with the loss of almost all lives.

In the evening, despite the weather, Inser went riding on Albrecht. It was dark before she returned. She had been to see Opa in the new farm.

I put on the embroidered apron for Klaus to see, despite his protest that he would see it on me when he came to the island. I know he will never come there.

146

That night, the four of us sat upstairs. Antoine sat apart, speaking to no one, reading *The Sea Around Us*. His face was haggard, his nostrils pinched, his lips set. Had he not been there or had he behaved naturally, we should not have been unhappy. Klaus, Inser and I sat together in the glow of the small lamp. Inser leant across my knee making idle scribbles in Klaus's sketchbook. She asked if she might read aloud portions of this journal, to test her English. I let her read part of the account of Andreasberg.

Before Klaus sent Inser to bed, we said goodbye to her, because Antoine and I will not see her in the morning; she has to leave early for school. After she had gone to her room, Klaus went to the bookcase and brought out a daybook he had kept in the Russian campaign. He turned to a drawing of an old woman sitting in front of a stove. I recognized it from a description of a Russian stove in one of his first letters after the war. Next, he showed the plans of campaign, a diagram showing the advance on Orel, and the retreat to Kessel. A drawing showed how he had escaped from encirclement after being wounded.

I drew his head in profile. At first he lay relaxed against a cushion; he then sat bolt upright as if he had forgotten where he was.

Had he been leading his soldiers across a frozen lake, had he been listening to the ring of boots on ice? Was he dreaming that we were seated together in the charcoal burner's hut, looking towards Thuringen Wald? Or was he with Brita?

Seeing him thus sternly absent, I realized for the first time, with what a difficult character I was engaged.

147

When we were alone, Antoine and I talked together for many hours, in great agony of spirit.

"What are you going to do about it?" he wanted to know.

"What do you mean, when you ask what I am going to do?"

"You and Klaus."

"We shall do nothing. There is no question... you shock me. I am going home with you."

"What if he comes to you in three years' time, and says he cannot go on with Helga, and wants you to be with him?"

"I should not go. I had not thought... your suggestion shocks me. We are already too close. It would be unbearable to be any closer."

"The trouble with you is, that your soul is too big."

"No soul can be too big."

"I have lost you — you are far away from me. I do not know you. Why did you not tell me before, about this?"

"There was nothing to tell; we were friends, close friends. That was all. You made this tension between us."

FEBRUARY 2

THERE was a feeling of others in the house being restless besides ourselves. In the middle of the night, Oma came out onto the landing, and went downstairs. It seemed that hours passed before she returned; but she was up again at about five o'clock to get breakfast for Inser. I heard the child's fresh young voice raised in the pitch-dark house.

148

We made an early breakfast. The ground was white; snow was again falling.

I climbed up onto the driving seat beside Klaus; I was wrapped to the ears in a fox-fur-lined greatcoat of his over my own coat. On my head, I wore his oldest and dirtiest hat, the one he uses for feeding the pigs, with an old scarf tied round it, and fastened under my chin. Klaus was delighted with my rakish appearance and declared that I looked like a Pomeranian lady.

It was snowing from the north, across our eyes. Antoine crouched, stiff with despair, behind us, looking as if he rode to his death. Albrecht, under the stimulus of a twig broken from the Schäferhof hedge, became swift and nervous in response to Klaus's mood. We passed over the level-crossing, into the Obernburg avenue. Albrecht swerved out across the road, and ran towards a woman on a bicycle, almost putting the shaft into her body.

We clattered over the bridge into the courtyard. Heads appeared at open doors in the servants' quarters. No doubt there were whispers: "The mad ones have arrived."

Leaving our coats inside the front door, we went through the main hall. In the sudden warmth, our faces became dewed with snow water. We called on Helga, whom Klaus kissed formally. Then he hurried away. The twins ran eagerly to the child-gate closed against their father's retreating back.

Helga invited us to take morning tea with her in Sophie's sitting-room. In a blue dress and white shawl, pouring tea from a silver teapot, she sat under an oil painting of her grandmother, to whom she bore a painful resemblance. She was polite.

She said: "You go back to England this evening?"

149

"Yes, but first we have to find out whether the trains are running in Holland, and whether the ships are crossing to England."

"This afternoon, I shall come home. I am anxious to get the children away from here: it would be terrible if they were to fall ill. Now, we will go to Selma. What a pity I did not have the opportunity to see your Sankt Andreasberg notebook. Have you seen the daybook Klaus kept there?"

"No."

"How strange. I thought you would have seen it... Cousin Sophie has invited you to stay for lunch."

Klaus was sitting in the Hastfers' apartment, talking with Selma and her mother. His face became set when he saw Helga. There were words between them; he rushed out of the room, and she followed him, without explanation or desire to be excused.

On the ground floor, Klaus was a long time telephoning through to the Hook of Holland to find out whether the ship would be sailing. He came back with the news that the first crossing of the North Sea after the inundation would be made this night.

Klaus was carrying his daybook which he had brought to the Obernburg for his mother to see. On the page descriptive of the Lapp hut was a drawing of the interior; two figures were sitting before the fire, a man and a woman.

"Come! We are going home, back to the Schäferhof, for lunch. First, you must say goodbye to my father. My mother is still in bed."

Herr von Ravenstadt was sitting in a dark drawing-room whose walls were covered with family photographs. He had

150

a rug over his knees; on the table before him was a tray with wine and glasses. The morning newspaper lay open before him. After inquiring about his health, we asked what news there was of the inundation.

"It is bad, a disaster. The loss of life is fantastic, and the damage to land is enormous."

"Fräulein Elizabeth, Herr Antoine, your healths. May you reach England in safety."

There came a timid tap at the door. It was Helga, her face tear-stained, looking for Klaus.

"I have not seen him, Helga. He is not here."

Klaus rushed in a few minutes later, with his hat and coat on, to tell us that we must leave at once. The three of us went down into the hall. Without a word to explain the change of plan, Klaus removed his coat and hat, and preceded us into the dining-room. Lunch was almost over: Helga, Sophie's companion, and two young men who had been at the hare shoot, were at table. Of the two men, one was he who had spoken so bitterly of old times, at the hare shoot; the other was he who had carried the hunting horn at his back. Helga's face was still tear-stained. She gave a quick glance at her wrist-watch as we came in. She pressed the bell for the maid. We shook hands with those at the table in an atmosphere of freezing embarrassment. The maid brought in a dish of eggs, and vegetables were handed round by the lady companion. Helga played with her fork. I took one look at Klaus's face, and averted my eyes. His features were hard, his chin was up. He threw out an arrogant remark at the tall sly man.

"She thinks the place will fall to ruins if she is not there. Now it is the turkeys ..."

151

I kept my head down over my plate, as did everyone else with the exception of Klaus. Helga said grace at the end of the meal; and with the white shawl pulled round her arms, the ends hanging down to conceal her pregnancy, she got up heavily from the table.

We put on our coats under Klaus's urgency, said goodbye to Helga in case she did not get back to the Schäferhof before we left for the train, and went for the last time to Selma's, along the haunted corridors. As I was passing Helga's sister's room, the husband was just going in; he paused to kiss my hand. I ran past the door of Klaus and Brita's old apartment.

Putting on a leather jacket, Selma came down into the yard to see us off. Albrecht became restive as I stepped up into the wagon. He reared, plunged forward, backed violently into the shafts. He tried to dash to the right, so that he was almost at right-angles to the cart, but Klaus was at his head, holding him. I bent down over the foot-board to lift the reins that hung in loops over the wheel. The young men with whom we had taken lunch stood by with expressions of amused surprise on their faces. I looked down at Selma, wanting to fix a mental image of her face, to carry with me into the future. We gazed at one another for a long time.

Selma stood waving to us under the heavy archway. As he whipped the horse into a trot, Klaus laughed, close to my face.

"We are running away."

Children were on their way home from school. They tried not to laugh at our odd appearance; at Klaus's crouching figure and bespectacled face deep in a fur collar like an arctic dweller; at me in my huge coat and scarf-anchored hat; at Antoine sombre in black coat and beret, hunched into the creaking wicker chair.

Pale sunlight showed up thin snow patches on the hills beyond Löhne. Once, Klaus turned round to look at Antoine.

"Are you well? You are very silent."

Antoine's only reply was a shrug of the shoulders.

As we turned onto the path beside the large Schäferhof, we saw Klaus's cousin, who inquired after the sick at Obernburg.

Oma met us on the doorstep, to tell us she had made a fire in the stove upstairs. Klaus left us, to return to the main road to meet the bus on which Helga's old nurse was coming. She is to stay here until after the confinement.

At three o'clock Helga, Anni, and the twins arrived. Helga had thrown off her distress of the morning, in pleasure at once more seeing her old nurse.

When he came in at coffee-time, Klaus's face looked thin and grey; the customary easy laugh and smile had gone.

At last it was time to leave. Opa and Klaus went ahead through the wood, carrying our luggage. Antoine and I followed with the rest of the gear. Helga came last.

"You must stay with us again in three years' time. Perhaps by then we shall be in Schlotheim," was Helga's farewell.

In the bus, Klaus said: "You have forgotten your cyclamen."

"It does not matter." The white petals were already dead.

On the station platform, as I kissed him goodbye, I thought:

"How old he sometimes looks. His hair is quite grey."

"You will visit us in England in the summer?"

"I will write."

"If you do, I shall come and meet you in London."

"I will write."

He drew me aside, so that Antoine should not hear him: "By summertime, I shall still be alive, if only a little."

"The sun gives me life. I shall store it up, and share it with you when you come. Remember me to Selma; I love her."

"Selma and Kurt are my good friends."

"Goodbye."

"Farewell."

From the train, because it was night and moonless, we could see nothing of the waters that had overrun the earth.

"He asked me why I was always laughing. He did not laugh today, did he?" said Antoine, in a low voice.

"No."

"So his plan failed after all."

We crossed the frontier into Holland. The guard opened the door of our compartment.

"Please, be prepared for an emergency. We are approaching Utrecht, where the train will be diverted to the Hague: please be ready to alight immediately the train stops. Motor buses will be waiting outside the station to take you to the Hook."

It was a cold drizzly night, but the wind was losing its force. Occasionally, between rows of houses, as the bus rattled over the cobbles, we caught sight of water. Red Cross

154

vans stood at the kerbsides. Not a solitary figure walked in the street. The bus drew up at the quayside. Very few people were travelling. We climbed the gang-plank; it was like going on board a doomed vessel. I went up to the steward in the passage outside our cabin.

"Will this ship cross tonight?"

"Yes madam, we are sailing, and we are going to Harwich, but after that, I don't know what happens. They have been badly hit on the English side, too."

"I am going up on deck," said Antoine; but he found the stair leading to the deck had been roped off. So there was nothing to do but to go to bed. Antoine took the lower berth: I slept in the upper one. The engines began to throb; a gentle sensation, a pulse-beat, then a creaking ran through the ship. We were putting out into the North Sea. I thought of how different our out-going had been at Christmas: of how the Dutch girl had stood under the deck-light, her hair a shower of gold. At this moment, she might be tossing on the monstrous waters, the wonder of her hair become a tangle of salty weed.

Klaus's face was printed on the night at sea. In the long darkness, his eyes watched over me. The vessel began to pitch and shudder; she rolled sideways. I lay awake, aware of silver schools of fish; and of limp-clawed lobsters killed and brought to the surface by the submarine cataclysm; of salt fathoms, of the meaning of sea-fathoms, of fathoms deep; of swaying plants; of under-water mountain ranges. The ship bowed from stem to stern; she began to roll heavily. I slipped outwards to the rail of my bunk as the ship shuddered at her utmost leaning into the seas; slowly, she righted herself, and fell away on the other side. My hip came in contact with the cabin wall, then with the bunk-rail. I turned over onto my back, and lay relaxed.

The confusion in my mind gradually cleared, and I began to trace my life back over the years to the first days with Klaus. How could I not have realized until this night on a storm-tossed ship that I had, as a girl of twenty, given my soul forever into his keeping?

TRANSLATIONS

p. 107: The quotation is from Sonnet 9 by Louise Labé (c. 1522–1566):

> No sooner does my bed softly induce
> Me to the sweet repose for which I long,
> The spirit from my body breaking loose
> On wings of sorrow flies to you headlong.
>
> (Graham Dunstan Martin's translation, 1973)

p. 113: The lines are from Rainer Maria Rilke's lyric narrative of 1906, *Die Weise von Liebe und Tod des Cornets Christoph Rilke* (The Lay of the Love and Death of Cornet Christoph Rilke):

> Riding, riding, riding, through the day, through the night, through the day.
> Riding, riding, riding.
> . . .
> Is that the dawn? Which sun is rising? How big is the sun? Are those birds? Their voices are everywhere.
>
> (B. J. Morse's translation, 1947)

p. 142: Chamberlain quotes again from Rilke's *Die Weise von Liebe und Tod des Cornets Christoph Rilke*:

> On the tree seems to curl
> a body, turning and twisting – a girl
> naked and bloody
> who shrieks: "Set me free!"

(B. J. Morse)

Introduction by Damian Walford Davies

Professor Damian Walford Davies is Head of the Department of English & Creative Writing at Aberystwyth University. His latest volume of poetry is *Witch*, which followed *Suit of Lights*; and his most recent work of criticism is *Cartographies of Culture: New Geographies of Welsh Writing in English*.

BRENDA CHAMBERLAIN
An Artist's Life
Jill Piercy
£15.99
ISBN 9781906998233

In this full-length biography of Brenda Chamberlain, Jill Piercy chronicles the life of an artist and writer whose work was strongly affected by the places she lived, most famously Bardsey Island and the Greek island of Ydra. She produced a compelling body of work, including the imaginative chronicle, *Tide-race*; the novel, *The Water-Castle*; the memoir, *A Rope of Vines: Journal from a Greek Island*; two collections of poetry; the play, *The Protagonists*; and her account of the making of the Caseg Broadsheets.

Jill Piercy draws upon extensive research gathered from manuscripts and journals in public and private collections and from interviews with Chamberlain's friends in Britain, Germany and Greece, which allow her to piece together the life and work of this complex and fascinating creative individual.

A ROPE OF VINES

Brenda Chamberlain

£7.99

ISBN 9781905762866

A beautiful and personal account of the time spent by Brenda Chamberlain on the Greek Island of Ydra in the early 1960s.

Sea and harbour, mountain and monastery, her neighbours and friends are unforgettably pictured; these were the reality outside herself while within there was a conflict of emotion and warring desires which is also vividly brought to life. Joy and woe are woven together in this record: the delight of a multitude of fresh experiences thronging the senses, the suffering from which she emerges with a new understanding of herself and human existence.

Both the intensity of the writing and the eloquent line drawings make *A Rope of Vines: Journal from a Greek Island* a distinguished achievement.

THE PROTAGONISTS

Brenda Chamberlain

Edited by Damian Walford Davies

£9.99

ISBN 9781908069962

Lemon, venetian vetches; orchis, fritillary. How hard to remember an olive tree when the soul is behind bars.

Never before published (and never performed since its staging in 1968 by the Welsh Drama Studio), Brenda Chamberlain's distinguished play *The Protagonists* is a major contribution to Welsh theatre, and to women's writing in Wales. Written 'at white-heat in three weeks' in autumn 1967, the play is Chamberlain's response – both heartbreakingly lyrical and disturbingly visceral – to the right-wing Greek Colonels' Coup of April 1967, which drove her back to Wales from Greece. *The Protagonists* represents the dark culmination of her profound, career-long exploration of imaginative freedom and the social role of the artist. It is also a startlingly candid dramatisation of her own emotional and psychological imprisonment at this time.

LIBRARY OF WALES

The Library of Wales is a Welsh Government project designed to ensure that all of the rich and extensive literature of Wales which has been written in English will now be made available to readers in and beyond Wales. Sustaining this wider literary heritage is understood by the Welsh Government to be a key component in creating and disseminating an ongoing sense of modern Welsh culture and history for the future Wales which is now emerging from contemporary society. Through these texts, until now unavailable or out-of-print or merely forgotten, the Library of Wales will bring back into play the voices and actions of the human experience that has made us, in all our complexity, a Welsh people.

The Library of Wales will include prose as well as poetry, essays as well as fiction, anthologies as well as memoirs, drama as well as journalism. It will complement the names and texts that are already in the public domain and seek to include the best of Welsh writing in English, as well as to showcase what has been unjustly neglected. No boundaries will limit the ambition of the Library of Wales to open up the borders that have denied some of our best writers a presence in a future Wales. The Library of Wales has been created with that Wales in mind: a young country not afraid to remember what it might yet become.

Dai Smith